1

Of Trails and Transitions

Transitions

A Collection of Isaac Green Stories

Thomas Ramseyer

Cover design by Hina Arshad @hinaarshad900

For Laura, for Everything

Contents

Introduction

Sadness comes as part of the package of living. How to deal with it, survive it, and perhaps even leave it behind can seem an overwhelming and unending enterprise. But with luck and intention, sometimes – in others, in beauty, in creation, in contemplation, in openness – one can emerge from sadness into a season of unexpected newness and light. May peace find its way into all hearts and minds.

Thanks to the human heart by which we live,
Thanks to its tenderness, its joys, and fears,
To me the meanest flower that blows can give
Thoughts that do often lie too deep for tears.

– William Wordsworth

Crossing a bare common, in snow puddles, at twilight, under a clouded sky, without having in my mind any occurrence of a special good fortune, I have enjoyed a perfect exhilaration. I am glad to the brink of fear...

In the wood, we return to reason and faith...

In the tranquil landscape,...man beholds somewhat as beautiful as his own nature.

— Ralph Waldo Emerson

When our world-deafen'd ear

Is by the tones of a loved voice caress'd,

A bolt is shot back somewhere in our breast,

And a lost pulse of feeling stirs again.

The eye sinks inward, and the heart lies plain,

And what we mean, we say, and what we would, we know.

— Matthew Arnold

Bent

(August 2017)

Only three deer today, and they were all in the first few hundred yards. Often he saw them spread throughout his near-daily saunter, but today, a slightly later start, they must have already cleared from the trails. The first two, does, together, were fox-red with tan ears and brilliant white tails perked high as they bounced away into nearby cover. He wished he had had his phone ready for a photo. He wondered how Franz Marc would have painted them – red, feeding on the ground; or perhaps blue, frozen in mid-air? Hiking nearly always inspired him, and lately, he needed inspiration. His recent failure to get anything constructive done perturbed him. So the early deer sighting was augury – "This is going to be good," he whispered. The absence of footprints in the fast-fading dew told him that the trails had not yet been trod by other hikers; that, too, was good. Squirrels were busy, frenzied even, and it surprised him that they failed to bark at his approach. They just scampered and jumped tree-to-tree or skittered through the grounded leaves. They had too many beechnuts and pine cones to attack – he was insignificant.

Isaac Green leaned into his walk, feeling the sun's growing strength as he headed southeast. The flannel over-shirt would come off soon, he knew. After weighing the many options, he had selected the Foothills Loop, a four and a half mile trail with solid footing throughout and minimal elevation variance. He wanted to stretch his mind beyond the trail, to be able to write or paint fresh ideas as they developed without worrying about his steps or breath. His daypack was light, maybe twelve pounds, most of that being his easel and paints – plus his iPad. A few light snacks and some water for later rounded out his load.

Painting had only come to him two years ago. Abby had helped him get started, and at times now, it seemed the only thing that helped, when even writing failed. His canvases were of nature scenes – objectively quite good, especially more recently. His technique and vision had steadily improved, and he now had a sizable collection of his own work – maybe three dozen decent ones. He had considered selling or pitching Abby's paints and gear, but he opted against it and was now glad he hadn't. He kept her studio in pristine condition, as she had, and it was still fairly full of her work, very different from his. Abby's paintings were more complicated in subject, often scenes of scattered images at odds with each other. His favorite showed a festive Christmas cocktail party, packed with joyous people. But interspersed throughout the canvas were various saints as partygoers, in the position of their martyrdom – Peter, nailed upside down on a needle-less Christmas tree, deftly straw-drinking wassail with a young businesswoman;

Dennis, holding his own head so that it could, in turn, bite off the head of a gingerbread man; etc.; all of them celebrating the birth that would lead inexorably to their own deaths. Isaac Green loved his wife's paintings, but he avoided that kind of intellectual quagmire in his own. His thoughts were just as painful, complex, and hard, but expressed in simpler ways. At the first real climb on the trail, he found that he had passed nearly a mile, not seeing anything but his wife's face. "Dammit." He wiped the single tear away before it left his eye, and mounted the rise.

A mile later, he arrived at Jacob's Landing, an overlook with a wide rock platform. He was hungry but wanted to get set up before eating. He wriggled out of the pack; pulled out his easel, camp stool, and paints; and organized them at a good viewing point on the outcrop. Then he looked over the valley in front of him. "Yeah." He was content. The morning had settled into a blue sky dotted evenly with white-gray cumulus clouds. He remembered

O'Keefe's "Sky Above Clouds" paintings – this looked similar, but his perspective was inverted. The sun, now high, created great huge cloud-shadows across the goldening-green Hannicutt Valley below. After a moment's contemplation, hunger returned to him. Prosciutto and provolone rolls, pita chips, and water made his snack-meal. He wolfed the first roll in two bites, then breathed and scold-chuckled, "Jesus, slow down!" The chips and the second roll were better, appreciated, after his self-disciplining. While eating, he scanned the area, eager to find something that caught his imagination. The valley colors changed too quickly with the shadows – his eyes and mind couldn't keep up. The granite pile from an ancient avalanche off left was a good subject, and it lay in great light, but he wanted something alive today.

A breeze had risen – nothing threatening, but enough to give movement to every plant and tree in the landscape, the pines creaking and whistling low and loud. Looking after the sound up and right, he noticed two young jack pines, bent permanently and to the extreme, one just slightly larger than and above the other. He studied the curves of the trees slowly, carefully. Although nearly thirty feet tall (or long, to be more accurate), they were dwarfed and darkened by the surrounding pines; they seemed looking for another way, parallel to the ground. The larger one remained vigorously green-needled, just bent, leaning over the smaller one, which was clearly weaker. "How the hell?" The littler bent pine bemused Isaac Green. Was it bent by heavy snowfall the previous year? Had it grown too tall too quickly and just bent under its own weight? Was it simply collapsing, too delicate to compete with the sun-greedy titan-trees? After several lengthy examinations of the area, his vision kept returning to this little pine. Apparently, this was it...his subject for the day.

He began by getting out his iPad and typing a few notes – a sort of descriptive plan of attack:

"Make big trees darker, thicker, aggressive. Extend the extreme branches of the smaller trees farther – arms reaching for sunshine. Blur the surrounding undergrowth – think Turner-esque. No animals. Companion tree should be just..." After listing more than a dozen ideas he thought important, his gaze fell again on the littler pine...for a long, long time. She had fought so hard, suffered so graciously. "Fucking life," he grumbled and picked up a brush. His first strokes were always his boldest, longest, bravest, and truest. After the background and main subjects, the remaining details came more slowly; he had to plan them carefully. He increasingly hesitated on successive moves, but he persevered, forcing strength where his impulse was indecision. He scowled, "C'mon, Hamlet!"

After an hour, he caught a second wind, and an unusual clarity came. He worked rapidly and continuously. The thinking and the list were done now. His hands were in a regular flow, moving from physical world to palette to canvas world – that trio on repeat. He held his palette in the sun, for he liked the way the paint felt, spread, and mixed in that warmth and glow. The colors glistened there, abstract rainbows, it suddenly seemed, on that piece of wood. "Double rainbow, all the way!" he whispered. God, she had laughed at that video. Isaac Green smiled and continued working.

The painting now quickly took shape, and by mid-afternoon, the details were complete, but for final touches. The trees had distinct personalities, and it was clear which were tragic, heroic, and villainous. Winners and losers were likewise obvious, same as in the human world. But in oils, the little tree – she would at least always stand a chance. Courage is curious, and we all get a chance to find and show it sometime. By 4:30, he found himself packing for the return hike. His painting had stood drying for over an hour. He now hung it outside his pack and let it bounce in the sunlit air back to his pickup parked at the trailhead.

Home, a cold Octoberfest poured, he cleaned and stowed his supplies, then revisited the painting. He frowned, then shrug-sighed. He had hoped for something more glorious today but was nonetheless pleased; despite its darkness, the painting spoke good and strong. Before he hung it to cure, he turned it around and Sharpied the title on the back edge of the canvas, tacked across the frame – "Cancer, #26." After a long draft of beer, he recounted the day. The beautiful does, the squirrels, the clouds, the little tree, its partner, the painting. Then he thought of the third deer, still a fawn, but barely. Spots just fading, it was too naive to be afraid. When he first came upon it, it stared, frozen, at Isaac Green for a full minute, then took a few tentative steps toward him, until the two does jumped out of the brush to get the young one's attention. They all dashed off without a trace. He remembered again thinking, "This is going to be good." And, all-in-all, it was.

Blood and Idiocy

(February 2017)

Eighteen degrees and still. Isaac Green stood for a moment in the clearing and took in the circle of grandeur around him. Towering beech and red oak trees dominated this flatter, lower section of the East Marbury Wildlife Management Area. Above, on the sides of the mountains, great sweeps of aspen gradually mixed and then gave way to the mature spruce and fir which lined the higher altitudes. From this small meadow in the valley, he could see a distant mountain lined with ski trails, some eight or ten miles away. Focusing back on nearer environs, Isaac headed east across the meadow and back toward the trees.

He knew this forest well – had been hiking here since his youth. It was sprinkled with a network of trails, so that even bushwhacking, one was never more than a mile from a trail in any given direction. This between-trails is where he found himself now. Despite the signed charge against such pathlessness, he loved to get off the track when possible, and he found it easier to do in the leafless and largely vineless underbrush of winter – unless, of course, the snow was too deep. Today, there was a fresh coat of early February powder about four inches deep, with solid, frozen earth below – perfect footing for hiking. He had left the trail a half mile to the west, and now wandered east and south toward the mid-morning sun.

Barely a quarter mile back into the woods, Isaac Green spotted the obvious line of a game trail ahead of him leading straight east from the meadow toward a small unnamed creek bed which he knew lay near the base of a sizable ridge line. He loved to find and follow game trails, as they occasionally led to great wildlife viewing opportunities. As he approached the trail, he noticed immediately that it was sprayed with blood, bright and fresh this morning – last night's snow blanket was thoroughly splattered. A single set of deer tracks accompanied the mess. He followed the trail northeast toward the creek, in the direction the tracks pointed. The scarlet stain on the snow intensified quickly, and it didn't take long for it to come to an end – a young whitetail buck, recently antlerless, lay in a pile, tripped for the last time by a fallen beech bough just off the game trail. He approached the deer carefully, as he knew the danger of wounded hooves. It was quickly apparent that the buck was indeed dead, and Isaac stepped up to it slowly but surely.

The slug's large entry wound was mid-gut, eight or nine inches below the spine. Several organs were likely destroyed – but not heart or lungs – and several arteries struck. Isaac Green crouched and reached out to touch-check the buck for freshness; it was still a bit limber and not really cold yet – could not be more than an hour dead. Anger rose in him as he stood and looked back up the trail and surveyed the area. Season had finished in November (or was it December these days?), so this young buck was definitely illegal. As a former hunter, he understood the temptation one might feel, especially with an empty freezer or unfilled tags, but that was no excuse – the prescribed seasons have for a century preserved both the herd and the hunt. He knew that the shit-head would be coming soon, as it would be impossible not to find this blood trail in the whiteness of the snow. Not armed himself, Isaac did not immediately know what to do – stay and confront the poacher or leave the deer to inevitability.

As he stood contemplating his quickly-disappearing options, Isaac Green heard a shotgun blast from about three-quarters of a mile to the south. Seconds thereafter it reported again, and then again. Silence followed. Three shots were, he knew, universally acknowledged as a distress call, used only in emergencies. Already half-knowing what had happened, Isaac Green set out at once in the direction of the sound. It would not take him long to get there – ten minutes maybe. Because of the closeness of the sounds and the lack of underbrush, he was fairly certain of, and could almost picture, the vicinity of the shots' source. Heading back up the game trail, he followed it to where the blood trail entered it; then, at the split, he followed the blood trail. At about a half-mile, he started calling out. Within another fifty yards he heard the response. Up the incline toward the top half of the ridge he found the hunter – clearly an amateur, probably from Albany or its suburbs – leaning against an oak trunk, holding his left knee. He was burdened with way too much equipment: a giant 10-gauge shotgun, a 45-ish caliber sidearm strapped gunslinger-style low on his right leg, the biggest prepper's backpack that Cabela's sold, and an over-abundance of ammunition stuffed in the shell loops of his brand new, still-store-creased hunting jacket. What the hell kind of harvest was he thinking he'd get – a whole herd? "Idiot," whispered Isaac Green. He shouted to the man to sit still and heard him somewhat sincerely "Thank God"-ding at his approach.

A quick examination told Isaac that the leg was not broken, as the man was sure it was. His knee, however, had become dislocated when the man tried to run down the hill after the wounded deer. After settling the jerk down – making him drink some water, and taking off some of the ridiculous gear with which he was still laden – Isaac Green told him what he was going to do. Although he had never done it himself, he had seen several knees relocated in his life, and he had a clear idea of what needed doing. When the man was ready, Isaac pulled his leg down while pushing the lower leg and kneecap back toward center. It took more pressure than he thought it might, but he heard and felt the knee pop into proper position as the unusually high-pitched scream escaped the poacher's throat. Not really wanting to gloat, Isaac

Green nonetheless took a bit of pleasure in the asshole's pain, and he smiled in spite of his half-hearted efforts to resist doing so.

The man – Mark something-or-other (who cared?) – now seemed genuinely grateful that he had been found, and that his new savior understood a few basics of emergency care. After making him drink some more water, Isaac Green collapsed the man's two sparkling new trekking poles to use as splints for his leg. He tied them on with some of the over-abundance of spare straps from the backpack.

Knowing that a side trail was just over a quarter mile south along the brow of the ridge, and that that trail led to the main path toward a ranger station, Isaac Green got the man to his feet, tested the security of the splints, and gathered the scattered gear. He then led the man down the ridge to the small route along which the buck had come. When they came to the end of the blood – the spot where the animal was struck – the man said something about the buck, asking Isaac Green if he had seen anything of it. "No. Stay quiet." was the end of the conversation. Several times, the man cried out obscenities as he stepped uncomfortably along the narrow path.

When they reached the established hiking trail, Isaac Green propped the man's backpack against a large aspen, maneuvered him into a somewhat comfortable position to sit, and got him a snack and more water out of the pack. After situating him and telling him to "Stay put and stay warm," Isaac set out quickly east up the track to where it met the main trail. Turning southeast, he covered the mile and a half to the ranger station quickly. Tim McKee, a thirty-something ranger whom Isaac knew fairly well, was on duty. After hearing the tale, McKee quickly called EMTs and conservation police, telling them exactly where to meet; he then locked the outpost, and they walked together back to the man.

Arriving again at the still-whining poacher, Isaac gave McKee his phone number in case he or the conservation officer had any further questions. He then headed down the trail without a word to the poacher, on his way back to wait by the deer. Arriving at the wreck, he pulled out his thermos and had some coffee along with some cheese and chips. Within an hour, he heard footsteps approaching. "Pretty hard to miss, eh?" called the conservation officer as he approached.

"No kidding – it's a mess."

"That bastard is lucky you were out here. Seems like I come across morons like him more and more lately," scoffed the officer. "Seventeen hundred and fifty dollars to the state, plus his hospital bill – maybe he'll use what little brains he has next time." The officer reviewed the story with Isaac Green and took some photos of the deer and the bloody game trail. "You can have the deer if you want it. I'm not hauling it out." Isaac didn't answer, but offered the officer a drink of coffee. "Thanks, but I've had too much already today – supposed to be cutting back on caffeine. Well, Tim gave me your number. I'll get in touch if I need anything else, but it's not likely. Pretty straightforward." After thanking him again, the cop took one more look and shook his head, then turned and headed back from whence he had come.

Isaac Green sat for a few more minutes with the dead buck before taking out his pocket knife and cutting a small cluster of hair from its tail. He tied it into a bundle with a blade of sedge, stuffed it in the front pocket of his small daypack, organized himself, and looked for nearly a minute back along the blood-stained game trail. Then he looked off to the west and struck out cross country in that direction instead. He knew that in winter, meat was scarce, and that the coyotes and coywolves would recycle most of the deer. Crows, eagles, and foxes would polish off the carcass. He recrossed the meadow, and at the depth of the valley, he again stopped and surveyed the surrounding mountains, which stood beautiful and unmoved by the insignificance of the blood and idiocy which had taken place below them. Isaac Green sighed a huge cleansing breath and headed back into the western slope forest toward the path that would lead to his truck in the trailhead parking lot.

The Color of Happiness

(December 2018)

Isaac Green just couldn't seem to get it right. He had started with the brightest, most vital colors – greens, pinks, yellows, azures, etc. He chose the most obviously uplifting subjects – flowers, a sunrise, even a stupid rainbow, which he always hated. They all left him flat. No combination of bright shiny subjects would express the joy that he so wanted to show. Inside him, he felt that it was bursting forth uncontrollably, so he tried to create that via a bouquet of buds coming to bloom, or the clearest of suns exploding into a perfect morning. But it seemed somehow false, too orchestrated or something, and he couldn't seem to put his finger on what the problem was. So, with a shrug-smile after three futile hours of attempts and a hopelessly ugly "pretty" canvas, Isaac put away his painting kit and closed up the studio – he had to get away and outside for awhile.

The clouds shifted back and forth in waves from light gray to slate to charcoal, and the air looked and smelled constantly on the edge of rain – maybe even snow. He couldn't really believe the 38 degrees on his little zipper thermometer; his skin told him it was much colder than that. Hiking was easy on the nearly flat out-and-back Meadow View Trail, located on the western side of a shallow valley, halfway between his house and Branbury. The trail was empty on this frigid and damp day, and he relished the natural solitude. He set a fairly fast pace in keeping with the ease of the trek and with his happiness. Isaac Green had no idea what woke him today with the interior smile that, though still persisting, had frustrated him artistically that morning. He needed to solve such problems. He hadn't been used to this feeling of contentment and joy – at least not for the past few years. If he could put his finger on its origin, he knew he would be able to write it or paint it. But for now, unable to come up with a reasonable answer to the color-of-joy question, he decided he would just empty his mind and enjoy the walk.

Light flurries came and went for awhile mid-afternoon, but Isaac Green knew they wouldn't last. The sky had gradually lightened, and the clouds even showed slight signs of breaking up. All afternoon, he had heard-then-seen huge flocks of geese beginning their trek southward for the winter ahead. They had remained a few weeks longer than usual with the abnormally warm weather of earlier this December. Now they crowded the exits all at once, barking and honking their way to nesting grounds in far lower latitudes, and their distant occasional cacophony would soon give way to a pristine silence. The forest was opening up and darkening, the leaves now nearly gone from most of the deciduous trees. Despite the loss of the fall color, Isaac Green was pleased to see the firs and spruces sifting their deep rich greens once again through the now skeletal hardwoods. As he approached Grimm's Pond, Isaac heard some crackling followed by a gradual and somewhat sustained splash. Rounding a bend at the northeast edge of the pond, he searched the bank and saw a beaver pulling its quarry, a thin 20-foot long, freshly-fallen alder tree. The beaver swam toward the inlet of a stream, the 3-inch chewed base of the tree firmly in its mouth – shoring up a lodge or adding to a dam somewhere upstream.

A short quarter-mile north of the pond lay the great meadow, and the trail rose slightly, leading to a series of four CCC-era viewing platforms that gave the trail its name. His favorite was the last of them, as it curved back slightly to the east and offered a look at not only the meadow, but also of Grimm's Pond in the background. The simple but lovely meadow, surrounded by low hills that gradually grew into the Green Mountains a few miles to the west, now hung slightly below Isaac Green. Although the trail and its decks sat only about forty feet above the meadow, they still offered great viewing all the way across. Isaac Green found his favorite spot, a rock outcrop, slightly below and beyond the man-made platform, that had formed a sort of stone captain's chair – carved by water of old, a perfectly sized seat section inset about eight inches below the "arms" and "back." He had been here many times, yet it always surprised him how comfortable it was to snuggle down in there. The stone immediately reminded him that there was one small sharpish spot on the right side of the back, so he arranged his day pack behind him on that side and let out a comfort-sigh as he leaned back into the embrace of the granite.

In the late spring and early summer, the meadow was riotous with color and activity. Birds would sing loudly and manage the wind-sweep deftly to fly from grass to grass, sedge to sedge, willow to willow, searching for food and nesting material. Every leaf on every plant would be in motion from the near-constant breeze. The season's first wild flowers competed in a beauty pageant, the pinks always seeming to win out only slightly – the yellows held their own, prepared to take over the crown if the pinks failed to perform their duties. Now, though, the meadow was still. Hardly any green remained. Lighter browns had darkened under the dull skies and the precipitation of the fall-winter day. The song birds were gone, and the immediate silence left the area in a starkness that was gripping. If it weren't for the geese far above, there would be no real sound.

Isaac Green studied the scene intently, then squinting, focused on the area at the south end of the meadow, near its meeting with the pond. Geometric patterns and lines populated the meadow. He pulled out his binoculars to have a better look. He smiled and recognized what he saw as game trails, made by deer, beaver, coyotes, and other meadow creatures. Earlier in the year, these were not visible due to the lush flora which threw a blanket over them. He had trouble believing the intricacy and sheer volume of the network that sprawled before him. Isaac felt the warm glow of discovery flow through him as he reclined into the cold rock which now seemed a part of himself.

As he began to climb out of his stone seat in the outcrop, Isaac Green was surprised as he looked at his watch and discovered that he had been sitting there for nearly forty-five minutes, studying and contemplating the world below him. He climbed back up to the trail, took off and stowed his jacket, and put his pack on, ready for the easy two miles back to the parking lot. He looked up at the sky, which had been brightening for the past hour and was now starting to clear. Taking one last look down on the meadow, Isaac watched a beam of sunlight flash from high in the western sky, through the first true break in the clouds, and fall onto the meadow where it met the pond. A heron, gray-blue, glided directly into the transient shaft of spotlight, alit on the bank of the pond, and immediately began a studying strut along its stage of the water's edge, hoping for a snack. A shudder arose from somewhere in Isaac's spine, forcing another smile to his face and a sudden mistiness to his eyes. "Damn!" he whispered aloud. As he strode down the trail, he knew that he had been all wrong in his approach to painting that morning. Walking rapidly now, he was already in his mind choosing and arranging the darker hues which would populate most of his canvas of joy – various grays, deep greens, heavy-cold blues, and browns. He would have the entire scene painted before he ever picked up a brush.

A Meeting

(November 2018)

At first, he feared she was dead. She was so still, sprawled completely out, just off the trail, the thick bed of dried leaves seeming to envelop her as if she were lying on a mattress of dough. Isaac Green's first impulse was to run or call for help, but hesitating a moment, he instead hurried toward her. Her long sleeved canvas shirt, plaid scarf, and jeans appeared to be undisturbed, and from several yards away, he could see no blood, no obvious injuries. Had she simply fainted, had a heart attack, or was she simply asleep? When he was within a few feet of her, he noticed that a book lay in her outstretched left hand; slowing then, he cautiously trod into the thicker cover of dried and crunching leaves. Without the slightest warning, she sat bolt upright, wide-eyed with surprise and no small measure of terror. Isaac Green jumped back abruptly, now fearing that he might become the one lying on the ground with a heart attack.

After a few seconds of silence, he said, "Oh my God, I thought you were dead – are you all right?"

"Yes..." she panted, "You just surprised me is all!"

"I surprised you?! Christ!" He leaned forward, hands on knees, steadying himself.

When she realized that he was not a threat of any kind, she relaxed a little and began to chuckle. He was not immediately amused, but when he caught his breath, he too smiled at himself, and went down to a knee there in the leaves, a posture more conducive to conversation. "What, uh..., what were you doing there?"

"Just lying down in this little patch of sun. I've been hiking all morning, and the leaves just looked...inviting. I couldn't resist." She smiled, looking almost adoringly up at the sun. He found her to be pretty – not the striking kind of beauty that Abby had been, but pretty in that simple and natural sort of way that some women are. He guessed her to be 40-ish, maybe a bit older, and she clearly loved being in the sun that she now studied; her tan was dark, and her dark brown hair slightly streaked and bleached from long hours outside.

"Sorry if I scared you," she interrupted his musing stare and began to rise. Brushing the leaves off of her shirt back and pants, she reorganized her daypack, putting the water bottle and book (he never got to see what it was), carefully away. Then swinging the pack over her shoulder and quickly checking the time on her phone, "Well...I've got a meeting in Branbury at 2:30, so I'm afraid I need to head on. Are you sure you're all right?"

Isaac Green stood and was finally able to look and smile directly at her. "Yeah, I'm fine – a little embarrassed. Glad you're okay. When I first saw you there,...I'm Isaac, by the way." He extended his hand.

She shifted her phone to her left hand and shook his. "Jean. Maybe see you on the trail again. I'll try to be standing next time."

He nodded, and she walked away south along the path. He watched her go for a long moment. Then gathering his staff and pack, he turned left and headed north – he still had about an hour left to hike. Though the Lower Ridge Trail was a moderately difficult one, a five and a half mile loop with a few good climbs, he felt it to be easier than normal. It was a perfect mid-November hiking day – a completely blue and sunny sky, fifty-eight degrees. He self-consciously realized during one tricky descent that his mind had still been busy thinking about the incident with Jean. He felt he had been awkward and foolish in the brief moment that they talked. Even after the more than two years since he lost Abby, it still felt strange to talk to another woman, especially one whom he found attractive.

Isaac Green spun his wedding band on his finger, and realized that he hadn't even checked to see if Jean had one on. Why should he have? – it was a completely unexpected, unusual, and very brief meeting. Finishing his hike, he continued to play with his ring, and he wondered, not for the first time, but more strongly that ever, if it was time to take it off.

Cold

(January 2016)

He stood still and silent, facing a gentle rise of the trail, and exhaled a plume of white vapor, which floated for a moment and dissipated to nothing in the frigid air. The leafless trees are so quiet in the cold. Even in the midst of a breeze, the overwhelming sense in a frozen forest is one that yearns for silence. One cannot help but be the noisiest thing in the woods, walking on the layered leaves, ice, and snow. With practice, Isaac Green learned to identify and avoid the most crunch-prone footfalls. Untrodden, off-trail, fresh-fallen snow is the quietest – another reason to take Frost's route. Standing still and concentrating, sounds from the far reaches of the woods came to him quiet but clear as crystal, gliding across the snow: various individual birds, a rare squirrel's skittering, a stream flowing around even the smallest rocks, a buck scraping his itchy and ready-to-drop antlers, and the crack of occasional distant branch falls. Isaac thought on how these ever-present sounds would get lost in the leaf-and-underbrush filled seasons, but they seemed much more focused and important in the bare-branched winter.

As he hiked, Isaac Green always tried his best to be in the sensory present. He loved the sights, smells, and sounds of the forest. The silent stillness of winter forced him to be even more alert. He had long ago made an analogy about the difference between hiking in winter and hiking in any other season – it was the difference between walking into a cathedral and walking into a grocery store. The cold, spare, muted, and largely empty atmosphere leads its human congregants into an attitude of worship, meditation, and even adoration at the genius of the spare forest architecture. In the winter woods, the Victorian "more" gives way to the Modern "less", which, as Mies reminded us, is really more.

The morning was a bracing, clear 12 degrees Fahrenheit – much colder, and he would have decided to stay home. The sun and the stillness drew him out, though, and the woods rewarded him with a beauty only experienced by the brave. The hike was a bit more difficult today, not only due to the temperature, but because of the fresh six inches of new snow that had fallen late last night. Walking became a sort of chair-lift marching-style step, that was at once challenging and warming. Isaac Green found that he had to slow down his pace and de-layer a bit to avoid perspiring, which is never a good idea below freezing. How amazing, he thought, to be hiking comfortably in 12-degrees with only a light merino wool quarter-zip and a fleece jacket. Isaac couldn't help but smile as he stopped, turned, and absorbed the complete and tranquil embrace of the forest.

He had been hiking atop a low rise on the west side of a little valley, headed south into the sun. A large ridge lay a bit further to the west with just a small dip between it and his present location. Isaac knew that he could at any point go about a third of a mile east and pick up a trail back to the road where he had parked. For now, though, he was happy where he was. He didn't want to attack the high ridge, especially bush-whacking as he was, but he did decide to venture down into the little dell and follow it back north for awhile. Almost immediately after his descent, he noticed that the ground had been trampled by innumerable deer prints headed south. Although he could not easily see the actual track at the bottom of the snow, he knew that's what they were because of droppings and other sign left by the herd. He had once come across the trail of several coyotes in the snow. Their tracks were more like trenches because their bodies dragged through the snow. The deer, however, were tall enough to step, or bound rather, over it and leave only leg prints. Isaac had the feeling that they must have been running because the tracks seemed to go straight down and straight out, with only minimal dragging of feet.

Following the tracks north to their origin, he came across something unlike anything he had seen before. In the lee of a decent sized rock-face to the west, lay a group of about two dozen ovals, most about three feet by two feet, impressed into the snow. Some were simply on top of the snow, but most went all the way down to leaves. Not one was touching another; at least two feet separated even the closest ones. These deer had bedded down last night in this protected campground, apparently as the snow was falling – no tracks lay to the north of their little hotel. Isaac Green surmised that something had spooked them this morning, and they lit out southward, bounding as fast as they could.

As he had been standing still for several minutes now, Isaac noticed that he was starting to get a bit cold, so he took off his daypack and pulled out and put on the down puffy coat which he had removed an hour ago. At first, he just studied the beds from afar, pondering why they were all so separate. Wouldn't it be warmer if they lay closer together – shared body heat and all that? Then he carefully approached and noticed that there seemed to be a random arrangement of various sized ovals. Large bucks interspersed with does and fawns (nearly yearlings now).

Approaching one of the larger impressions, one which had absolutely no snow on its bottom, but rather a base layer of last fall's leaves, nearly completely dry. He knelt down next to it; then, looking around rather self-consciously, he climbed in and curled up, his back pressed against the side with the tallest snow. He felt himself enveloped in the bed, and knew that with the proper covering over the top, he could be quite warm in this cocoon. Each indentation worked the same way for the individual deer. Sleeping in closer proximity would allow the cold night air to come into their beds from not only the top but from the sides as well; hence the separation. Kneeling in "his" bed, which was nearly in the center of the group, Isaac Green looked around at all the other ovals and then stared south where they fled down the dell. He pictured their hurried-but-not-desperate departure, and for a moment imagined himself as the buck who had made this bed, monitoring them as they dashed away and occasionally looking up the hollow to the north to see if anything was, indeed, headed their way. When they were all gone, he would linger a moment, then turn and fly after them.

Loathe to leave, but seeing that the light was beginning to wane, Isaac reorganized his day pack and began to head north up the dell, but stopped abruptly. For some reason, he wanted to leave that area free of tracks. He made a sharp right and headed east toward the trail. Topping the small rise once again, he looked south down the valley, hoping to find a great stag of a buck staring back at him from a great distance. Nothing but trees, brush, and snow returned his gaze. The deer were long gone, safe for another cold night in another hollow in the lee of another cliff or hill. Just as he met the trail, he felt the sun that had been shining on his head disappear, replaced by the shadow of the great ridge. The cold sharpened around him, and Isaac picked up the pace for the last half mile. It was time to go and make his own separate cocoon in front of the wood stove at his house. Just before arriving at the road where the relative warmth of his pickup awaited, he turned back and opened his arms in homage to the glory of these winter woods. The great darkening forest lay before him silent and lovely in the still evening cold. Isaac Green felt alive and inspired and aware and happy and connected – and most grateful.

Enveloped

(September 2016)

Smoking a cigar always got him a little high. He leaned back in the porch rocker in the breezeless dusk, feeling the Cuban smoke swirl around and with him at every draw. Looking out at the mixed-wood forest, his head against the back of the chair, Isaac Green felt truly comfortable for the first time in a very long while.

Even though he called it "The Shack," his little cabin was really a quite substantial one bedroom timber-frame with a loft – small, but well-built and comfortable. Isaac Green had bought the property right out of college with his friend David when this kind of land was really cheap. The fifteen-acre unincorporated parcel adjacent to the Green Mountain National Forest was about a two-and-a-half hour drive from his home and in the middle of nowhere – his favorite location. The following summer, they put up the cabin in about three weeks with the help of Ricky and Paul. The four friends would gather there once or twice a year for deer or turkey hunting and cabin improvement work, but that tradition faded as careers took off and spread them all out. After David's sudden death, unmarried and with no family, the land and cabin came fully to Isaac. It became his retreat, one which he needed now more than ever.

Since Abby died, life had been a whirlwind of confusion and busy-ness. The kids, though adults with their own families, suffered desperately at the loss of their mother, and Isaac tried in his best dadly way to be there for them. His brand of loving stoicism, though comforting in some ways, was not always the balm that they needed; mostly, they just needed to be together and with him for awhile. They remained at the house for nearly a week after the funeral, under the guise of helping and comforting him, but really, he realized, because they didn't know what to do without their mom in the world.

They all occupied themselves with mundane tasks: reading sympathy cards, emptying Abby's office and studio at the college, going through and divvying up old pictures, writing thank-yous for memorial gifts, etc. One by one, they headed, with long hugs and many tears, back to their worlds, eventually leaving Isaac Green to face the future in a truly frightening ignorance. A little more than two months into trying and failing to get back any feeling of normalcy, he threw some clothes and supplies into a backpack, texted his plan to his kids, hopped into the pickup, and headed north to The Shack.

Evelyn, now seventy-three, was surprised but very pleased to see him, as it had been nearly a year since he had been there, that last time with Abby. She allowed Isaac Green to park in her near-empty barn when he came up there because no road accessed his property, which was squarely between her land and the national forest. When he approached her, she cried instantly and profusely, pulling him into a strong motherly hug that lasted a full minute. When he had called in late July to tell her about Abby, she was crushed but tried to remain stoic, clearly putting on a strong voice just for Isaac's benefit. Although Abby had only been to the Shack about a dozen times over the years, she and Evelyn had hit it off immediately – a childless woman and a motherless one, each filling the voids of the other with love and friendship, laughter and sympathy. Isaac did not realize how much he had missed Evelyn. She insisted that he come in for lunch before heading out to his cabin, and he did.

Two generous bowls of ham-and-beans and two large slices of fresh honey cornbread later, he made his way, against her repeated pleadings, out the door and toward the trees. At the forest line, he looked back to wave at Evelyn, who returned his wave, holding her other hand over her mouth to hide the little sobs. Mid-September is an exceptionally beautiful time to be in the northern Vermont woods, with just a hint of color-turning, and temperatures ranging from about 45-to-70 degrees. He found the little trail that they had made all those years ago, and as he walked, he couldn't help but look up at the canopy, quite a bit higher, it seemed to him, than it was just 130 miles south. Perhaps it was because his small trail was unused that it appealed to him so. Robert Frost would have said it "wanted wear." It seemed to beckon him into the depths of the forest, and he needed to be enveloped in something lovely – like Evelyn's hug and her home-cooked meal. Isaac felt happy to be surrounded with this, his preferred world.

A twenty minute casual hike found him on his property, and another two minutes took him to the shack. It looked at first glance to be in good repair, but it, like the trail, seemed to yearn for his presence – it needed just a little maintenance and sprucing. And he needed its needing him. Even before bringing in his gear, Isaac Green walked the outside-then-the-inside perimeters of the cabin to check for any real problems, and he found only a couple. The short section of gutter that he had installed over the back door steps was hanging by only a couple of nails – victim of a falling branch. Also, the chimney cap on the kitchen wood stove looked loose, and would need to be reattached a bit more securely. Isaac always loved that they had installed two wood stoves on opposite sides of the structure, one in the kitchen and one in the main room. The interior looked pretty much intact, with only a surprisingly small bit of mouse sign – a relief. He opened all the curtains and a few windows, started a fire in the main wood stove, and looked under the sink to check the battery connected to the single solar panel on the roof. It was fully charged, meaning he could have water and a few lights (if he wanted them), and the mini-fridge should work. When he plugged it in, it kicked on with a soft clunk-then-hum. A quick ladder-stair climb to the sleeping loft completed his inspection. It, too, was in good shape.

He set a kettle of water on the stove and began to unload his pack, putting food in the pantry box and the fridge, a few books and supplies on the kitchen table, and his few clothes in "his" drawer of the dresser in the bedroom. He had already decided not to sleep in the bedroom – too many memories of her in there.

Isaac Green always kept a rifle (a little antique pump-action 22 for squirrels or rabbits), an old manual typewriter, and a bottle of some sipping whiskey at the shack – his special items. Whiskey first. It was a nice smooth rye, and the first sip (actually a full-shot mouthful) felt warm all the way down, helping to relax and take his first slow, really deep breath in about a week. Isaac looked over at the typewriter on the shelf and shook his head at it – "Not this trip, old friend." He grabbed the rifle from the loft's floor joist where it hung and, sitting in the armchair next to the now-crackling wood stove, inspected it all over. It looked clean but for a little dust. He pumped the chamber open to let some light in so he could take a look down and into the barrel. Also clean, but might do with oiling. He laid the gun across his lap and had another sip of the whiskey. He looked over to the old cracker tin on the kitchen shelf where he knew he had a supply of bullets, then stared at the stove awhile, his mind now active.

The sound of the water boiling brought him back to the now. He stood, rehung the gun back in its place, and went to the kettle where it steamed on the stove. He moved it to the warming arm, and put the small cast iron frying pan on the direct heat, adding a spoonful of ghee. A minute later, the ribeye he had brought was sizzling in the pan. Isaac poured some of the hot water into the French press, already supplied with coffee grounds, and poured some more into a small bowl of Idahoan instant potatoes (extra buttery flavor), stirring them vigorously for a few seconds. Salt, pepper, and a ripped-edge chunk of the baguette he had brought completed the meal. He took pride in both the taste and efficiency of the whole project; even cleanup was quick and easy.

Moving back from the sink to the living room, he passed the bedroom door, turned in, and stepped up to the dresser again, and picked up the framed five-by-seven photo of himself, Abby, and their kids from about fifteen years ago – God, they were all so young and full of life. Now, he felt the years. Replacing the picture, he looked down at "her" drawer for several seconds; then reaching out, he opened it hesitantly, hopefully, and a bit fearfully. It was empty but for a pair of socks hiding in the back corner. These were her absolute favorite extra thick and oversized woolies, light blue with fox faces scattered all over. She would put them on on chilly evenings, and he remembered her wearing them the last time they were here together. She had asked him to bring them to her at the hospital, and he had scoured their house looking for them, to no avail. With apologies, he brought her a different pair – nice, but not THE ones. Isaac took the socks out to the chair in front of the stove, took off his shoes and socks, and slipped into Abby's. Holy shit, no wonder she loved these. They were easily the softest, most comfortable, and warmest socks he had ever put on, and the slightly snug fit felt wonderful. He sat for a moment, just feeling them – feeling her.

Isaac Green arose and refilled his coffee mug, leaving room for some rye at the top. He grabbed a cigar and the coffee, and headed out to the porch rocker to finish his evening. Wiggling his toes inside of her socks, he cut and lit the cigar, getting a good cherry started. The coffee blended well with the tobacco flavor. His mind became a blend of memories, projections, and fears, as the intoxicants of the cigar, coffee, and whiskey began to do their work. He felt at once happy and guilty for being happy. His pain at her loss – his loss – was immense. His desperate love for her remained immeasurable. Could he go on without her? Yes. But did he want to?

Taking another sip of the coffee blend and another pull on the cigar, Isaac Green, settled back into the surround of the chair and rocked gently back then forward. He would remain there warm and comfy in Abby's socks for another forty minutes, finishing the smoke and thinking. The butt had gone cold, and so had the dregs of coffee. With a deep sigh of regret and resignation, he at last answered himself aloud, "Yes...eventually." He went inside, closed the door, stoked the fire just a bit, and reminded himself of the chores he needed to do tomorrow. He walked past the bedroom door, taking a long glance in there, then continued on and climbed the ladder to the loft. He glanced at the rifle, hanging ready in its place, as he climbed, and fell into bed and under the heavy down comforter, a deep and dreamless sleep awaiting him.

Wild

(June 2018)

He had almost stepped on it, but with a last-second recognition of something unusual underfoot, he hopped to the side to avoid destroying it before getting a better look. Isaac Green now squat-straddled the muddy narrow trail at its crossroads with a game-trail and stared down at the track in the muck. Definitely canid and headed in the same direction as a deer track not a foot away. He often saw dog tracks out on trail, but they almost always went in the direction of the trail, not perpendicular to it. He also knew that this print, at about five inches long, was far too big to be a dog or a coyote. A thrill of excitement shivered its way through his entire body. Every year, he would hear and read stories about wolf sightings in the state, but rarely were they verified. He took out his phone, carefully placed his own foot just to the left of the track for reference, and snapped the photo. Taking a few steps down the game trail, Isaac found an even clearer print and photographed it likewise.

This trip to The Shack had brought him more wildlife sightings than usual – deer, marten, turkeys, two foxes, and even a solitary bear seen at about a half mile across a small valley – but he had never even hoped for this. He knew that the chances of actually seeing a wolf here (if indeed that's what this was) were minuscule, but even just finding the track amazed and excited him. After several minutes of studying and photographing the print, Isaac Green continued down the trail, which now headed back toward his cabin about a mile and a half away. The remaining twenty minutes of the hike seemed like only five as the image of the track and the idea it represented filled him with wonder...and, for some reason, hope.

It had started to rain, quite unexpectedly, on his return to The Shack, so Isaac changed into a dry shirt and threw together a quick lunch of bread, cheese, and summer sausage. He also rewarmed the coffee pot on the wood stove to take off the chill of the rain shower. Before he sat down to eat, he grabbed his copy of Aldo Leopold from the bookshelf – he had suddenly remembered the great essay about wolves in that collection, and he wanted to read it again now with the image and idea of the paw print fresh in his mind. The cheddar bit sharp and delicious as he scanned the contents page, quickly finding "Thinking Like a Mountain." It was a fast read, beautifully crafted and profound. Far beyond just a text about the wolves-and-deer relationship, the essay expressed (and arguably introduced to the larger populace) a holistic view of the connectedness of an entire ecosystem, and even a way of viewing the great earth and our place in and on it. He ate and read slowly and with relish. Meal and essay completed,

Isaac Green wondered if the smile he now wore was from contemplation of Leopold's idea or the satisfaction of the lunch.

Isaac's afternoon of small cabin repairs went smoothly. The rain had been replaced by sun even before he ate his lunch, so he climbed onto the roof, took down the bent top section of stove pipe (damaged by a falling white pine branch), and easily straightened out the dent on his splitting stump using a piece of firewood as a hammer. While up there replacing the pipe, he cleaned some accumulated leaves and needles from around the solar panel. In the back corner of the open-air woodshed, he had kept a stack of some remaining siding shingles that David had cut and split by hand when they first built The Shack. Isaac Green located them and grabbed five or six of the best ones he could find to replace a few that had begun to rot in the back near the base of the cabin – best to take care of this now, before they completely disintegrated. To his relief, only four cedar shingles really needed replacing, and that job, too, was done in a flash, the spot of the shake bandaid standing out bright and fresh with color. That would change quickly, and it would all look a uniform grey-brown again by next spring. He felt happy with and proud of the fairly meticulous work he and his buddies had put into the original construction of the building. That extra effort had made maintenance simple for him ever since.

Through his two hours of projects, his mind kept coming back to the idea of the wolf tracks. He wondered about the size of the wolf's territory and where it lay and whether it was a lone wolf or part of a pack. He also mused smilingly whether wolves had domestic "chores" to do, like he had just done – likely not. The paw print and the wolf itself stayed in his mind as he made the short trek over to Gray's Lake, less than a mile away, just into the national forest. He wanted a swim, but he also hoped to catch a fish for dinner. Fish first. Using a tiny ball of bread slathered in bacon fat, he cast his line out, but not too far from shore. He was hoping to get a bullhead or an inquisitive smallmouth. Almost immediately, the bait was taken. He could tell it wasn't a huge fish, but it might make a meal. As he pulled it close to shore, he saw that it was a crappie, and a fairly good sized one, much larger than his hand. He put it on a stringer and quickly re-baited, re-cast, and hooked another, even larger than the first. Those two would work nicely for his dinner. He cleaned the fish, put the four small filets in a ziplock bag, and disposed of the guts and heads back into the lake for the other fish and the otters.

About fifty yards north, there was a great swimming spot with good-sized rocks for jumping in and climbing out. It was cold, almost too cold, but in the clear afternoon summer sunlight, Isaac Green felt good – totally alive and free and wild – as he swam straight out into the lake and floated naked on his back, taking deep relaxing breaths half on top of the clear water. He dried himself in the sun on the warmth of a flat granite slab before heading back to The Shack.

Sitting on the porch of the cabin two hours later, Isaac savored the taste of the fish along with the potatoes and onions fried in ghee and bacon grease. He looked out and into the darkening dense green forest in front of him, and thought about the wolf track and the animal that had made it. He wondered why it persisted so in his mind. Why did we always enlarge "the wolf" in our lore and in our collective psyche? Why were we at once drawn to and fearful of the creature and its mysterious ways? Leopold wrote of seeing the "fierce green fire" in the wolf's eye. Wildness. Untamedness. Naturalness. Complete freedom. The antithesis to domesticity. The wolf seemed to represent what we have lost as a species – the trade off for culture, comfort, and intellect. Isaac wondered if it was a good trade for us and whether we could ever trade part of it back – just a little of it. Throughout his life he had often sought to do just that through his escapism, his writing, his painting, his choices of how to be a husband, a father, a citizen, a creature of nature. Seeing that paw print this morning just forced to consciousness where and how he lived. Were his attempts to "get back to the Garden," as Joni had put it, effectual at all? He pulled out his phone to look at the photos. There the paw print lay, in the same mud, on the same trail, in the same forest as his own foot. The kinship was clear, but with one difference – the insulation of his boot. For Isaac Green, this image explained it all, and he sighed at the awareness. He knew that no matter how much any of us tried, we would always be somehow separated from that original and pure connection to the world of the wolf, the wild. But the effort, every action taken in that direction, seemed to him to be a noble and holy one. After about a half-hour of quiet meditation, pondering, and melancholy musing, he rose and gathered his plate, cup, and silverware, perfect symbols of domesticity. Just at the doorway though, he froze, silent, and turned back, listening. Goosebumps rose over his whole body, and his ears seemed to stretch far into the forest, waiting and wanting. Then, faint and distant, it came again. No more than a whisper, but distinct and unmistakeable, the long low lingering howl of a single wolf.

Fluorescence

(July 2016)

She was not made for this light. The horribly
garish fluorescent inundation flooded the ward and
every room in it. It was relentless and unforgiving.
Every hurt, every facial expression – an attempt at
a brave smile, a wince, or a frown of fear – was
magnified on purpose by that light. The medical
necessity didn't make it right. It did not belong on
her and she did not belong in it. Abby belonged in
the glow of her studio, the sun warming the whole
of the space through the south-facing glass doors.
This room had no yellow or orange tones – only
cold blue hues and an unrealistic white. Isaac
Green hated her being in this place, he hated that
his wife and friend was dying, and he mostly hated
that inhuman, humming, frigid light touching her,
his Abby.

It was last January, only six months ago, when Abby had first told him that she thought something was wrong. Isaac Green could tell by the concerned tone in her voice that it would turn out to be awful, and he wondered how long she had actually been covertly ill. In their nearly twenty-seven years together, she was rarely sick, and never with anything serious. The only time she had been a patient in the hospital, other than for the deliveries of their children, was when she had to have stitches about twenty years ago. She had been experimenting in new artistic media and decided to see what she could create with plywood and a nail gun – a two-inch framing nail shot right through her hand. He had teased her that it was her half-realized stigmata. But this past winter, when they went in to get her checked out, Isaac Green did not even attempt to tease. Her look told him that she was already leaving him.

Her diagnosis came in early February. Pancreatic cancer, stage four, likely spreading quickly. After two months of intense chemotherapy combined with radiation, attempts to shrink the tumors in order to do surgery, things were only worse. Cancer was found in her lungs, her liver, her...well, pretty much everywhere. Treatment was halted much to Isaac Green's angry dismay, but Abby was done with it, and the doctors said continuing would not give her much more time in exchange for the pain it would cause. Though she had fought valiantly and had outwardly hoped that something might come of it, she said she knew deep down that the treatments wouldn't help, even before she had started the first course.

A certain relief came with the resignation. Abby felt better for quite a while after the chemo stopped. No more nausea and much more energy. But she was still sick, still dying. Isaac Green noticed some subtle changes in her personality over the next few months – no, not really her personality, but her preferences. She was eclectic in her artistic choices but had always been a sort of disciple of the magic realists, surrealists, and fantasists. Now, however, she found a renewed love of Georgia O'Keefe – could not get enough of her. Likewise, she had always listened to Mahler religiously, but had mostly focused on his younger works: "Wunderhorn," the first few symphonies, etc. The second was always her favorite – how she would glow when the chorus entered with the first pianissimo "Auferstehen." Now, she would hear only "Das Lied..." and the Ninth. He noted similar shifts in other areas, too: A move from Wordsworth to Keats, from Fitzgerald to Hemingway – Isaac Green had teased "better late than never" on those two. Her real personality, however – her humor, her love of just about everyone, her compassion, her beautiful smile and the heart it reflected – none of those ever flinched, not for a single moment, even to the end.

One perfect day in late June, Abby was feeling especially well. Strong enough to walk with her cane out into her studio. Isaac Green brought her some tea then left her basking in the warm incandescence of the sunlight shining in on her, "Der Abschied" softly infusing the studio, her finger on a page of Shelley's "Adonais" resting on her lap, her eyes closed and a sweet smile lilting on her face, her head leaned back against the rocking chair. As he stood in the doorway, observing her on his way out, he thought, "My God, she looks so beautiful! Has she always been this beautiful?" In his heart, and in her soul, yes, she was always perfect and radiant. But objectively and physically, his mind finally conceded that, no, she had not. Not when they were first in love, not the day they were married, not in her pregnancies, nor any day of her motherhood. Not when the kids graduated high school or college, or when they, in their turns, got married. This perfect day in late June was her most overtly beautiful day in her adult life, and Isaac Green felt as if he were a sort of apostle, grateful to be bearing witness to the miracle that she was on that day, and wishing he could share his testimony of her glory right then with the desperately wanting world.

Two days later they were in the hospital, and would remain there for the next week. The change was swift and drastic and devastating. To ease her pain, she received regular and heavy doses of opioids, and they blunted everything. He had hoped that she would rally for a day, an hour or two, a half-hour even, but she didn't. She had already left him. The kids had come there for a couple of days, and he had sent them home just the day before; they planned to return on the next weekend. Now he was truly on his own. Abby lay there inert and fading, the monitors beeped, the vacant fluorescent lights hummed, and Isaac Green, holding his wife's mostly limp hand, sat stupefied by it all.

The end came quickly as he knew it would, but too, too soon. At dawn on the Fourth of July, Abby's breath became confused and then stopped abruptly. It took the doctor and nurse what seemed forever to get in there and shut off the fucking machine that screamed incessantly from the moment her heart and breath stopped. They checked her pulse, and as this was expected and planned-for, just sighed, unhooked all the wires and cables, offered what seemed like their sincerest condolences, and left the room. The sun was half hidden by a cloud but was rising elegantly into the low sky. Isaac Green, not really knowing what to do, slowly and numbly got up, went to the door, and shut off the overhead lights. Abby lay motionless as the growing warm beams of the morning's glow shone in on her face. Looking down at her, Isaac Green once again took her hand, sat down on the bed next to her, and said "There you go – that's better." Then he ran his thumb over the old scar and smiled at her as his silent tears crashed down onto their hands.

Phoenix

(April 2018)

It sort of snuck up on him. Isaac Green suddenly found himself on a burned-over hillside. It caught him off guard because he had been hiking for awhile, and the trail had lain in perfect, typical mid-Spring conditions: tree buds' gold-greens giving way to darker, richer hues; a few flowers and grasses sifting their way through the leaf litter on the forest floor; the bird song growing from a Haydn quartet to a Mahler symphony; the squirrels climbing up-and-down, digging, and barking. It had been the first full week of the spring without any rain except for a light overnight sprinkle. The trail felt wonderful underfoot and was completely mudless. But now, only forty minutes in, he was surrounded with ash and the smell of the burn. He could not tell exactly from which direction the fire had begun, but it must have started fairly low on the ridge because the whole side looked burned, and it had to have happened in the last two or three days.

Nearly halfway up the ridge, the trail turned back sharply to the east, and he knew it would eventually lead downward toward the unburned area near the river from whence he came, but curiosity made Isaac Green step off the trail and begin climbing the hillside to the northwest. He had never been in such a freshly burned country before, and it fascinated him. The scorched earth and the bases of the trees were covered with salt-and-pepper colored ash which lay lightly, not moving in the calm mid-morning except where he stepped, each footfall sending a pair of mirrored curling ocean-waves around the sides of his hiking shoes. Isaac's senses were fully engaged now, as newness demands attention. The smell was strong and strange but not unpleasant. It had a bite to it that the aroma of pure wood smoke did not, which told him that it was mostly the underbrush and ground debris that had burned. The trees, mostly pine, wore scaled skirts of black bark at the bottom, gradually giving way to their usual gray-brown about sixteen inches up the trunk – definitely charred, but not permanently scarred. The canopy showed no sign that a fire had ever occurred.

A five minute's hike further, and he came across a long dead log still ablaze on the ground. In actuality, it mostly smoldered, but a few flames still danced on its wider end where deposits of resin had gathered at the junctures of the trunk and the first remaining branches. Isaac noticed, not five feet away, that a delicate yellow trout lily had shoved its way through the blackened leaves and was nearly ready to bloom. He thought of the last two years of his life: Abby's sickness and death, the sharp feeling of loss, of loneliness, of emptiness. He thought of the times when he seemed to be walking a fairly steady path, only to find himself scorched by a memory or a hope gone up in flames. Still, he found a way to keep walking; his pathless route was just different now, and steeper.

For the next ten minutes Isaac Green was adrift in the burn. No patch of earth in his field of vision remained untouched by the fire, and, overwhelmed for a moment, his breath heaved, and he briefly had to lean against a tree. Forcing a deep slow breath, he calmed himself. Though the burn enveloped him now, he knew it could not go on forever. He climbed. The hillside inclined more steeply now, so he often stopped for brief rests. Looking back now and then, he saw clearly that the up-ridge side of the each tree was increasingly less charred than the down-ridge side. The fire must have either picked up speed or lost strength as it raced to the top. Reaching the summit of the ridge, Isaac smiled in both physical and mental relief. The climb was over, and he now saw that the fire had not carried over to the other side, which was awash with spring brilliance. Isaac felt as if he had opened the door to Oz, into a dazzling world of previously unknown or long forgotten color, more glorious than he thought possible. Greens, yellows, whites, and pinks blanketed the hillside below him. He smiled hard and felt his eyes well up in joy and in affirmation.

Turning right, Isaac Green followed the ridge line back to the east for about a half mile, color and verdancy on his left, grayscale and dormancy on his right. He walked the curved and narrow line between Yin and Yang. Could you truly appreciate one without consideration of the other? His mind worked. Was someone to blame for the fire, or was it naturally lit? How long before the burn scarring normalized? Would it really be possible to completely return to the way it was? As he continued along the ridge toward a smoother descent point and the end of the fire line, the image of the trout lily in the forest flowered again into his mind. Isaac stood still and looked again to the right and then to the left, and he saw immense beauty on both sides. He at once felt an emptiness and the beginnings of a growth that might become fullness, and he somehow knew that emotional scars would heal, too. It was spring and blossoming time was nearly here.

Town

(December 2018)

When he thought of town, Isaac Green had mixed feelings. He tended toward Thoreau's dictum that "in wildness is the preservation of the world." At the same time, he really did feel that innate human draw toward other humans, and he knew the somewhat arrogant pride in how people had wrested habitations from the immensity of the natural world. We had indeed paved paradise for some parking lots – Joni was right; nonetheless, some of these pavings (like Paris or Florence) were fucking beautiful. Isaac had thus come to a self-negotiated truce that, for him, town was an occasionally necessary nuisance.

The first really cold day of early winter was on a Thursday in early December. Isaac Green decided the night before that he needed to head into Branbury to buy some groceries, get a haircut, grab a few art supplies, and head to the hardware store – he always found something to buy there, whether he really needed it or not. He hadn't seen Andy and Donna at their cafe for a couple of months now, so he went in early to have breakfast and see how they were doing. Habit took him to his usual booth. From there, he knew he could see and talk with Andy who stood over the flat-top grill frying the eggs, ham, pancakes, and hash browns that flew out to tables and booths around the restaurant. Sadie, the spitting image of Donna in her younger years, was his waitress, and when she saw Isaac, she shouted to her mom and dad across the cafe – they both turned and yelled their sincerely happy greetings to him, but could not stop their work to come over. Isaac tossed his usual jab at Andy, "Still slacking off, I see!" He had always taunted Andy that he just stood in one spot most of the time while his wife and daughter scampered all over the cafe. It was good talking to them all, and

Isaac was glad to see and hear that life was good with them. They had all pretty much caught up on things by the time his second refill of coffee came, followed shortly by his ham omelette with American fries and rye toast, so a busy silence settled while he enjoyed the first few bites.

Finishing the last of his breakfast, Isaac Green was just about ready to shout to Andy about how good the omelette was, when a shadow over his shoulder passed by his booth and went to the next one, facing away from him. She wore some sort of uniform-casual attire, dark slacks and a khaki shirt – he had only seen her standing for a second before she slid into her booth. Her hair was about shoulder length and dark brown. Sadie stopped by and topped off his cup before moving on to the woman's booth. He saw her turn over the woman's cup and fill it with coffee as she said, "Hi, Jean! What can I ..." And that was all Isaac Green heard of their conversation.

He nearly jumped as Sadie nudged his arm and giggled, reaching for one of his empty plates, "Everything OK, Mr. Green? You look like you're in another world!" He laughed with her for a second before lying, "Just thinking through my to-do list for the day." His heart beat quickly as he stared at the woman sitting in the sunlight just six feet in front of him. He wondered if it could be a different Jean than he had met awkwardly on trail about a month ago, but when Andy hollered a greeting to her and she turned to look at him, Isaac Green clearly saw her pretty smile in profile, and he recognized her voice as she teased Andy, "I see you're still letting Sadie and Donna do all the work around here." She and Andy laughed together at their evidently ongoing joke, before shouting to both Jean and Isaac, "I feel like I'm being ganged-up-on this morning – first him and now you!" Jean turned briefly to see whom Andy was referring to before returning to her coffee and the newspaper she had brought in. Not five seconds later, she spun full around, a look of recognition, pleasure, and humor on her face. "Isaac, right? I think we met on one of the Ridge Trails a few weeks ago!" Isaac smiled gratefully that she remembered him, but he also blushed at the embarrassment of that meeting. "Are you alone?" she straightforwardly inquired, and after his nod, "Wanna join me?"

Bringing his coffee cup with him, Isaac Green sidled into her booth opposite her. He was glad she hadn't come to his booth for two reasons: first, he didn't want her to see his crumbs and the two breakfast plates that Sadie had not yet cleared, and he wanted to see her face in the sunlight rather than backlit as she would have been facing him in his booth. For a moment, they both just sat quietly and smiled. She was just as pretty as his memory had often reminded him that she was. They reintroduced themselves, recounted with laughter the clumsiness of their previous meeting, and tentatively made some small talk, during which he found that her last name was Buchanan. She worked as a forester for the U.S. Forest Service office up in Manchester – about a half-hour commute from her home here. As he took a sip of his coffee, he noticed her looking at his hand. "Is your wife meeting you here, or...?" When he told her that he had lost Abby about a year-and-a-half ago, she expressed what seemed to be truly sympathetic condolences. After a moment, she said, "It took me almost three years before I took my ring off." As she told him of her husband's death about five years ago, all his thoughts of fear, of doubt, and especially of guilt fled, replaced by gratitude. He felt his eyes mist up just ever-so-slightly, and he hoped she had not seen but knew that she probably had. Her gaze was soft but reassuring, and it remained on Isaac Green for longer than he could have wished.

Several minutes' worth of conversation later, he asked "Are you on your way to work?" She looked up at the clock on the wall behind Isaac, and with a start, said, "Shit – Yes, I've got to go!" A silent but mutual panic grasped them as they stared for a moment at each other. She quickly reached into her purse, dug around, and came out with a pen. She grabbed a napkin and wrote down a number. "Give me a call. I'd love to do this again," she said with a sad smile, then began to gather her belongings. Isaac Green nodded, stood, and offered her his hand as she got up. She took it slowly, gently, and happily. Before they let go, he was surprised to hear himself say, "I'll call." Jean turned to leave, and Isaac watched her. After she was out the door, Andy shouted, "You two know each other?" Approaching the checkout counter, Isaac said half under his breath, "Not yet," then got out his wallet and retrieved a credit card. His errands that day were pleasant, and the time seemed to fly. Hopping into his truck to head home, he reflected with a wistful smile that sometimes coming to town was not a nuisance at all.

Awakening

(September 2017)

From the tent, he could hear the loons calling in the early morning cool. His back was sore as hell. Isaac Green bet he had turned from side to side twenty times in the night – getting older is just plain painful. Happy at least that he had not had to get up in the night to pee, he groaned out of his sleeping bag and into clothes for the day. The loons continued their cries for another half hour as he found his way to the outhouse and back to start his little alcohol stove. Coffee was going to be especially nice this morning. An extra hint of autumn chill still hung around as the sun began its task of fog-burning a bit more slowly than usual – maybe it had had an uncomfortable night's sleep, too. As the water neared a boil, he got his cup and instant coffee packet ready. No one else was up yet, and Isaac had to wonder if they were sleeping more comfortably than he had, but he took a bit of evil pleasure in imagining that they likely had not – he almost felt guilty at the smile...almost.

Isaac Green had not been on a trek like this in decades. He had hiked consistently, at least weekly, but not with a full pack of gear and supplies for six days. In his youth and early adulthood, he had loved backpacking. He an Abby had often gone out for two or three night mini-adventures, especially before kids; as their family grew, they had become more of a base-camping clan, largely just doing day-hikes. In the year since Abby had died, he had hiked more often in an attempt to help himself find clarity, space, and breath. He and a few old friends had for years talked about getting back on trail again, and, he assumed as a way to keep him occupied, they had quickly organized this trip. They decided on a nearly 50-mile section hike in the northern quarter of the Long Trail. While mostly a peak-to-peak hike, a few lakes dotted the trail, and they were all spectacular and clear. This campsite next to Rains Lake was a wonderful find – yesterday's hike, the second of their six days, was a brutal one, and Isaac Green was really feeling its effects on his I'm-too-old-for-this-shit body.

The boiling water made magic in his cup – the coffee, though just instant, smelled heavenly to his nose. Isaac strolled the thirty yards down to the lake with his mug and, with his free hand, roll-hobbled a log stump against a tree so he could sit and lean back. There he sat, the most physically satisfied he'd been in about ten hours, just watching the motionless lake, fog hanging in thick-then-thin horizontal layers on the far side only. The loons were at the borderline where the fog began – five of them motionless but moving. They and their calls gradually drifted out of sight and sound into and our of the fog. After about a minute or two of not having them there to entertain or occupy his mind, an overwhelming stillness enveloped him as he stared at the spot into which they had disappeared. No motion on the lake or in the trees; no sounds; not a bug, squirrel, fish, or leaf stirred. It was the first time Isaac Green could remember feeling so totally still, and so completely adrift. He felt at first like kicking his feet in the leaves, like clearing his throat, like throwing a rock into the lake. But he did nothing – just sat there and let himself sink into the void of stillness, fog, emptiness. He even closed his eyes and held his coffee away to let the circle of sensory blankness surround him more. It did. His heart slowed, his mind emptied, his self-ness, or as Emerson put it, his "mean egotism," faded, and his consciousness seemed to reach out into the lake fog toward something, toward everything, toward her. Though it only lasted a few minutes, it seemed like climbing out of a deep pit when he came back to encounter the physical world of his present place. Isaac Green assumed it was the smell and warmth of the coffee that pulled him back. Opening his eyes, however, he discovered, not more than six feet directly in front of him, a beautiful, fluffy, green-eyed fox peering directly into his face. It remained in this staring match with him for a full fifteen or twenty seconds before simply turning its head and casually trotting along the small lakeside game trail off to the right.

Looking out at the now nearly fog-free lake, he began to ponder the brief interaction with the fox and with the void, especially the moment of his initial inaction – his conscious decision to sink or drift off. What had he wanted from this stillness? Why did he let it continue? Where was it attempting to take him, and why was he going so willingly? How long had the fox been there before he noticed it? How strange and enormous is the abyss of one's own mind? Before he could really begin to delve into these questions, though, Isaac Green heard the unmistakeable rustle and zip of someone else waking and stirring. It was time to come back to society – to conversation and trail business. Still time for another cup of coffee first, though. As they spread out on the trail later, opportunities would arise to think more – about the morning's adventure, about connecting with life again, about Abby, and about finding his own place in the world.

Reflection

(September 2015)

Isaac Green had a tough time actually believing that it had already been twenty-six years. Time too often slips by unacknowledged, at least by our consciousness. Its physical signs abound – kids growing up and moving out, bodies moving a bit slower and with a bit more stiffness, touches of gray sneaking into hair once solid rich mahogany. These effects creep up, though; as John Lennon wrote, "Life is what happens to you when you're busy making other plans." Twenty-six years and-then-some of life had happened to him since he had met Abby, and for some reason, this anniversary prompted him to reflect on where it had all gone. What happens to time once it leaves your present? Does it exist somewhere aside from our memories? Is there some sort of separate dimension or continuum for the past? "I'm too damned metaphysical for my own good, sometimes – or just full of shit," he thought, almost laughing out loud.

In the truck on the way up to The Shack, Isaac posed it to Abby: Where did the years actually go? Sitting next to him, as she always did, on the bench seat of their old but still nearly mint F-150, she sighed and snuggled her head on his arm. "Hmmm," was her only response for quite awhile. He knew that she was either formulating a full response or falling asleep or both, so he remained silent, driving as she clung to his arm, the wheels in her head spinning just as fast as the truck's, now running up U.S. 7, just north of Rutland. But unlike the truck, her mind was going in a million different directions at once, taking her on distracting tangents. He knew she would get back to him with a proper response in her own time – she always did.

They had decided to head to the cabin for a couple of days to celebrate their anniversary. Most of the time would be spent just hanging out, relaxing, and/or doing some regularly necessary maintenance, but they would also do some hiking and maybe swimming if the lake was still warm enough this late in September. The real celebration, besides the wonderful surprise party the kids had thrown for them the weekend before, would be a trip to The Bough, a little-known but fantastic restaurant up west of Waterbury, overlooking the Winsooki River. It had been designed by a student of Frank Lloyd Wright's in the mid-40's, and Wright himself had added a few touches to the design. Abby loved the organic aesthetic of the place – truth be told, they both did. Additionally, the food was unbelievably good. Isaac Green always got the brook trout, fresh from the river, but Abby had ordered different meals in each of the five or six times they had gone, and she had never been disappointed. "Was she ever disappointed by anything?" he wondered, still waiting for her answer to his query about time. He would have to wait a few more days.

When they pulled into Evelyn's farmyard where they always parked their vehicle, the clock on the dashboard read 11:15 pm. Abby awoke and fluffed her hair as she apologized for falling asleep, which she always did when they travelled more than a half-hour anywhere. Evelyn had left the barn unlocked for them, as Isaac had warned her that they would be arriving late. After stowing the truck and re-locking things, they donned their packs and headed down the trail for the not quite twenty-minute hike to the cabin. They would come back to visit with Evelyn tomorrow or Sunday as she had likely been asleep since about 9:00. The nearly-full moon made headlamps unnecessary after just a few moments of eye-adjustment. Abby actually loved night-hiking, and this was an especially gorgeous night for it, clear and brisk, but not cold. Isaac, not realizing it, took off at a very brisk pace, and Abby made him slow down to enjoy the walk, feigning fatigue. He took her hand then, and the two strolled together along the nice wide path that he had cut many years before.

Arriving at The Shack, they spooked a great horned owl perched upon the ridge of the cabin. When it jumped into flight, it startled them both, but it truly seemed to frighten Abby, who let out a short shriek as she dropped to the ground clinging to Isaac's leg. He helped her to her embarrassed feet and asked if she was okay, but she only giggled and hurried the last few steps toward the cabin door.

Isaac immediately got the power hooked up, plugged in the fridge and turned on a few lights and the water pump. Although Abby usually liked to unpack everything as soon as they got there, the lateness convinced her to just stow the refrigerator stuff and to do the rest tomorrow. She went in to get ready for bed as Isaac lit a fire in the wood stove. By the time he came in, she had changed into an oversized t-shirt and her favorite comfy socks. She was tired, but she wanted to be with him before sleeping. They made slow, warm, satisfying love, and then fell asleep spooning in a twisted pile of arms and legs.

The next day, Isaac Green was excited to go for a good long hike, as they had planned, but Abby instead just wanted to go and have some "girl" time with Evelyn, since they hadn't seen her the night before. So they went their separate ways, planning to meet back at the Shack around 1:00 pm for a late lunch and then chores. Isaac took a small trail that skirted the east brow of the ridge upon which the cabin lay. It led him into National Forest lands, and eventually, he would take a right fork, heading down to a small mountain pond. The day was cloudy but comfortable, and he thought, smiling as he strode, of the night before: the drive, Abby falling asleep before giving an answer to his time question, her fright at the owl, her somewhat surprising late-night desire. At the pond, he was excited to find a large mature bull moose wading and eating water lily or pondweed or something, dipping his entire head under the water to bite-grab the plants, rising back out of the water to chew and swallow before going back down for more. Isaac watched him for at least a half-hour, quietly munching his own snack of Craisins in tandem with Teddy, his nickname for every bull moose he saw. The time passed quickly, and Isaac wondered if Abby's time with Evelyn was going by as fast as his – it probably was. It suddenly struck him as strange that some "times" seem to go faster than others. After all, an hour is an hour, no matter where you are or what you're doing, right? Why then should our perception of it alter depending on our experience? Teddy caught sight of him for a second, and stopped eating for a couple of minutes, staring and frozen in time, until deciding that this man posed no threat, he simply continued grazing. A fast-developing idea in his head, Isaac Green tossed his daypack back on and headed quickly back to the Shack, anxious to do some writing before Abby returned.

At about 1:15, the cabin door opened, and Abby entered, a bit spent from her rather brisk walk back from Evelyn's in the light rain. While she dried off and rested, Isaac put together a light snack lunch of crackers, cheese, carrots, and almonds. They wouldn't need much, as their reservation at The Bough was for 7:00, and they both wanted to be hungry for that. As they moved toward the table on the porch, Abby abruptly turned back into the cabin, holding up one finger and saying, "Oh...almost forgot." He saw her reaching into then producing something from her bag, wrapped in a cloth tea towel. He knew immediately and smiled, anticipating; Evelyn had sent a treat for them! She lay the parcel down in front of him, and he opened it quickly, revealing a beautiful large chunk of coffee cake, the smell of sugar, butter, and cinnamon wafting into his nostrils. He broke it in half, but she insisted that it was all for him as she had had a piece during her visit. Abby shared with him that all seemed good with Evelyn, who hoped to get to see Isaac before they left tomorrow evening. They ate leisurely, talking only occasionally in the quiet of the overcast calm. He loved the day thus far and wished that he could put it on a loop to play over and over – it seemed to be the definition of tranquility. The clouds and sprinkles persisted all afternoon, erasing any hopes for a swim at the lake – maybe next trip. They sat for a long while on the porch, watching and listening to the drops fall on the forest and the roof, postponing the chores for just a while longer.

Their dinner at The Bough was wonderful as always. The trout was perfectly cooked, and it came with mushroom risotto and a vegetable, which, as it was nearly autumn, was green beans almondine. Abby, after much travail, selected the pheasant, which was also spectacular, roasted and served with mashed sweet potatoes and the same green beans. A lovely Provençal Rose accompanied the meal. Isaac had requested a window table when he made the reservation, and the late summer evening offered a stunning view of the Winsooki, flowing not-too-far below. They had long ago given up the practice of giving each other cards, gifts, and flowers for their anniversary, opting instead for experiences together, like this trip and this dinner. They had, however, gotten into the habit, sort of jokingly at first, of giving each other little trinkets on their anniversary – tiny things that they had found or made one for the other last-minute. Dessert seemed the appropriate time for their item exchange.

Abby pulled from her purse an envelope and handed it to Isaac. It held a pencil sketch on a half sheet of paper. The little drawing, done just a few days ago on the back of a hardware store receipt, featured an Appalachian Mountain scene in the background, Isaac prominent in the center, seated in a large armchair – Lincoln Memorial style – and with several of his favorite accoutrements surrounding him: daypack, coffee cup, tent, pocket knife, iPad with keyboard, a few books and vinyl albums, and a woman (nondescript, but it could have been Abby) sitting topless on a tree stump stool immediately to his right. With his right hand, he cradled her left breast, and in his left, clutched his hiking staff planted firmly in his lap. A stocking cap sat lightly on his stolid head. In the bottom right corner of the sketch, just above her signature, Abby had written, "The Coronation of Isaac I." He spent a minute or two scouring the picture to see all of the details (reading the titles of the books and albums, noting her detailed work, etc.), his face beaming with pleasure. Grinning up at her for a moment and taking a drink, Isaac Green looked back down at the sketch and finally noticed the title. It was as if what he read had said "Cue Spit Take." Coffee spewed out and over the sketch, the remnants of his dessert, and the candle between them, snuffing it out. They both laughed aloud, wiping frantically with napkins, as they looked around the room to see how many people were staring – several. He finally calmed himself enough to whisper, "The orb and scepter? Oh my god, Abby – that's hilarious! I totally love it – thank you!" Their waiter came over, cleared plates, relit the candle, and refilled coffees, giving them a much needed pause.

When they were once again alone at the table, Isaac pulled out his phone, completed a few operations, and placed it on the table. A second later, Abby's message notification chimed. "I've gone virtual this year – hope that's okay." She swiped open her phone, half-expecting a link to a funny website, or even a plan for some hopefully not-too-distantly future trip. Instead, she found an email from him entitled "Time" with an attached document. She opened it and smiled up at him, seeing that it was a poem. Isaac Green had not written any poetry for years. It had always seemed to him a younger man's craft. He had grown into prose over the years, and he found it to be a more satisfying writing form in the long term, and definitely more lucrative. But this morning, upon returning from the pond, he found his writing outlet in verse. Abby read in silence, a smile on her face and in her eyes:

Time

In our youth, we fly; time crawls.

In our age, we slow; time races.

In our panic, time stands still.

In our calm, time evaporates.

In our sadness, time heals.

In our joy, time moderates.

Time had run on long before us

And will sprint on long after us,

As its marathon never ends.

Some say time is a river,

I say it is the memory of the wind.

You and I have sighed together in its cooling
     breeze.
We've sheltered ourselves against its buffeting
     gales.
We've longed for it in our personal droughts.
We've watched amazed as it curtains the tall grass.
Our time is short and precious,
And I am blessed to have passed mine with you.

Though so elusive and hard to hold,
This wind is ours, so let's be bold
To make windmills of our future days,
And harvest that time, before it us slays.
So let us attempt now, hard as we might
To freeze each moment, and clasp it tight.

     **Here's to the next 26 years!

     Love ya!

     Isaac

As Abby read, her smile gradually faded, returned, and faded again, ending in a quiver of a lip and a somewhat broken sigh. She uttered a barely audible "Thank you," and quickly got up, subtly pointing in the direction of the restaurant's restrooms and dashing off that way. Isaac Green was puzzled and a bit worried – he hadn't intended to make her sad or upset; in fact, he thought it was a sort of uplifting and hopeful look toward their future together. She wasn't gone long. Completely changed and looking composed, upright, and happy, she strode back to the table. On the way to her seat, she leaned in and gave him a quick kiss, apologizing and saying that she really loved his poem. After a pause, she explained – almost over explained, at a too-fast pace – that she had, for some reason, been quite emotional that day anyway; and that she wondered how much time she had squandered on silly things in her life; and that she was a bit worried about Evelyn living out there all alone, time passing as it must; and "yada yada yada," as she self-effacingly put it. He let her odd explanation pass, and simply raised his coffee cup to a "Happy Anniversary" toast, ending their beautiful dinner.

The next morning was spent in cleaning, closing things up, and packing. The cabin was put to bed for the winter should it arrive before they returned. As they stepped onto the path back to Evelyn's and their truck, Abby turned back to look at the cabin, saying "You know, you did a pretty amazing job on this little 'Shack' project." He suggested that perhaps they could get back up in the spring. She nodded and smiled at him, then turned quickly and headed resolutely down the trail. Evelyn, of course, had coffee and baked goods, homemade donuts this time, prepped for them when they arrived, and as always, the short goodbye turned into an hour of laughter and conversation. As Isaac was loading the truck, Abby remained with Evelyn, taking what he thought was forever to say her farewells. He tap-honked the horn, breaking the women's long embrace.

After an initial pensive silence in the truck, Abby became unusually chatty on the trip home, vocally observant of every beautiful or eye-worthy mountain, tree, or animal along the way. Having arrived in the driveway back home, she suddenly and a bit cryptically answered his nearly forgotten question about time from the other night. She said that the years didn't actually go anywhere, that she thought time was not like a stream or the wind, but it was like the air, surrounding us always, never really passing, but changing us as we inhale and exhale it, if we are willing. He shut off the truck and made a show of taking a slow, deep breath in-then-out, his eyes closed, asking, "Am I changed?" She shrugged 'who knows?' and told him to think on it for a few minutes, adding "but don't be too long. I'll be unpacking...in the bedroom." He watched her nearly skip into the house, backpack over one shoulder.

Isaac Green did think on it for a few minutes. "If we are willing...?" he thought. Does every moment offer us the chance to change in some way as we create memory out of time? Yes, he supposed so. This mostly cloudy weekend, filled with mostly mundane tasks and experiences, was for him, mostly joyful, and he would gladly be willing to be changed by and for these memories. Movement made him look up to see the curtains close in their bedroom window, bringing him back from his musings. He grabbed his gear, and he himself nearly skipped in to the house.

Scary

(October 2018)

Eleven a.m. on a Tuesday, and Isaac Green was out on trail – "God, being (semi-) retired is fantastic," he thought. It was one of those absolutely perfect mid-fall days, the surprise 'Indian Summer' after you thought real warmth would be gone for the next six months. Every leaf-crunching step told the deer to stay clear or down but did nothing to deter the squirrels in what might be one of their final days of good food and shelter prep for the upcoming long winter. Being a mid-week work-time hike, Isaac seemed to have the trails to himself. He had selected an area in the Green Mountain National Forest that he hadn't been to for quite awhile – about a half hour east and a little south of Manchester. The trail led south along Eagle Brook from Crop Top Mountain down past Eagle Brook Pond. South of the pond, Isaac Green would leave the trail, cut cross country to the east about a quarter mile, and pick up a section of the Vermont Long Trail that led back north to within a hundred yards of where he left his truck parked.

The sun was on him nearly the entire way. He was proud of the fact that he planned it that way – heading south on the east side of a ridge in the morning and north on the west side of the facing ridge in the afternoon. At 12:15, he reached the pond and found a little perch just off the trail to sit and have his lunch. The pond shone bright blue under the even bluer crisp sky that displayed only a few scattered wisps of cirrus ice fingers way high up. A hunter friend had given Isaac a couple of lengths of home-cured venison sausage, and he ate a few slices of that interspersed with chunks of a sharp cheddar he had picked up in Branbury the week before. That and some wasabi almonds made his lunch, and Isaac Green washed it down with some Cabernet he had loaded a skin with.

Now, sated and inspired by the view and the solitude, he felt like writing. As his keyboard for the iPad was on the fritz, he had prepared to go old-school on this hike, so he pulled out a new mini Moleskin and his favorite pen. Words flowed easily today, and the gist of a story came quickly. It was from the perspective of an anthropomorphized coyote ruminating on being an inadequate hunter. The coyote found that even though many other animals were afraid of him, he himself was even more afraid – for his mortality, for his obsequiousness to the wolf and bear, and for the survival of his family line.

Isaac wrote two solid paragraphs and a sketch of the rest of the story within an hour and a bit. He stopped for a second to shake out his wrist and hand when he realized that the sun was no longer on him, and that he had been at it for quite some time. Finishing his sentence, he packed everything up and continued south along the trail, skirting the pond. Just past the pond, he found a decent place to cross the distance east to the Long Trail section that he would take. It was a tougher little trek than he had anticipated, but after twenty minutes of scrambling and bushwhacking, he came to a clearly defined path that he knew had to be the VLT.

This section of the trail was quite flat, so he extended his stride just a bit. It felt good to stretch out his legs, and he was making really good time. After about a quarter mile, he came around a bend and realized he was quickly catching up to another hiker. As he got closer, he could decipher that it was a fairly short woman, and her gait hinted that she was likely older than him. Though not really labored, her step was just a bit clunky as with a bit of arthritis. She had no pack of any kind– just a side holster water bottle. She must just be doing a quick out and back hike to the pond from a parking area to the south. Isaac Green slowed. You never know exactly how to approach another hiker from behind so as not to startle them. He couldn't stay back here, as her pace would be uncomfortably slow for him – he had to pass her. As he closed the gap between them (now about thirty yards), he decided to cough loudly so that she might hear him and not be caught unawares. When he did, she turned her head momentarily, just enough to see him. She picked up her pace, but it was still too slow for him, and he guessed that she was straining to make even that speed. He decided he had to just rip the bandaid off, so he sped up to catch and go around her. She occasionally stole a quick glance over her shoulder at his figure, and she looked a bit panicked. He hated this feeling, being the object of fear for another person – especially a fairly vulnerable one. When he was within about ten yards of her, she suddenly stopped, stepped off the narrow trail, and turned to watch him approach. Isaac tried to smile, and he said, "Nice day!" as he went around her, but he could clearly see the real fright in her stare, a gaze which he could not bear any longer. He simply strode by as quickly as he could, looking straight down the trail ahead. A few yards down the track, he turned back to see if she was following. She was still on the side of the trail, her hands now on her knees and her head bowed down. He could imagine a series of deep panting sighs of relief coming out of her. Resisting the urge to turn back and go check on her (fearing that might only panic her more), he pushed forward, quickly moving out of sight of her.

A wave of guilt seemed to crash over Isaac Green, along with no small bit of anger. How could he, a man who tried his whole life to be kind and benign, be seen as a threat? What should he have done to be less frightening? Also, what was a woman who was obviously so nervous doing out on trail alone? ...and why the hell should he be made to feel guilty for simply taking a hike? The remaining two and a half miles back to the trailhead were a tangle of thoughts and emotions, still unresolved as he got into his pickup. What had started out so beautifully had turned into the scariest and least satisfying hike of his life.

Lonely

(June 2017)

When it came down to it, Isaac Green finally had to admit that, for the first time in his life, he was lonely. It was a completely foreign and disturbing feeling. He had always argued, a la Thoreau, that loneliness was a sort of self-imposed and egotistical emotion, that in spite of infinite solitude, one's mind could always connect with someone or something else in the world (a tree or an ant even) and avoid the feeling or concept of loneliness. But now, nearly a year after losing his Abby, he now felt its crushing pain.

All of his adult life, Isaac Green had loved time alone. Solitude had regularly provided him with means for inspiration – his walks in the woods, his extended times of observation and contemplation, his hours of self-communion , his reading, his silence – these kept him grounded and aware of his place in the world. "Getting away" (from the kids, Abby, society, or work) was never the reason for his regular search for solitude. It was just part of him, of who he was. Abby had gracefully, though with some occasional and obvious disappointment, accepted this trait of his from the beginning, and he loved her the more for her generosity and unselfishness of time. And he did so love her, truly and desperately.

For the first few months after she died, his kids had been too present and had kept him too busy for him to be anything even close to lonely. Hell, they barely gave him any space to even mourn in his way – by himself. For the rest of that first year, he would fitfully try to reorganize his life, clearing out drawers, boxes, collections, and closets. He had no real emotional issues with these items of hers. They were "things" she liked, studied, or wore, but for him, they were no real part of her. He didn't – wouldn't – change a thing with her studio, however. She was everywhere in there. He saw her vision in each of her paintings, her literal fingerprints on the brushes and rags, and her constantly-working mind on the palettes and sketch-book erasures. When he eventually began to use the studio more regularly, he still left most of it as it was, but for his immediate work space. So even after her death, she was still physically there throughout that studio.

Gradually, he gave more and more of Abby's paintings to the kids, and set several aside for the grandkids (some which she would never know) to have as gifts on special birthdays and events. A few he gave to the college where she had taught, and donated a few more to be auctioned at a local American Cancer Society event. His own art began to take up more and still more of the studio, and it seemed now more his than hers. He always kept a few of his favorites of hers hanging there. He mostly loved and kept her unfinished paintings and sketches – they helped him imagine her still working there in the place where she was most alive and happy. Although he did not know if she ever realized it, he would sometimes sit just outside of the ajar studio door, often for ten or fifteen minutes at a time, covertly watching her work. The range of feeling that she showed as she worked was astonishing – joy, contentment, illumination, pain, amusement, determination, frustration, sorrow, anger, pride. He smiled at the remembrance. These were some of his favorite memories of her...of them. Alone together, loving – truly and desperately.

One late-June day, not quite a year after her death, Isaac Green spent the morning in the studio working on a painting he had started the previous day. He worked intently for two hours, then set the painting in front of one of Abby's oils to dry. As he walked toward the door, he looked casually back at his works which now nearly filled the studio. He was happy with his progress as a painter, and thought back gratefully on Abby's attempts to teach him the basics of line, shape, color, light, and texture. Then scanning the room, suddenly stricken, he struggled for breath and nearly collapsed into the stool near the door. His eyes flew about the room in a frenzy, searched and searched, then filled with tears as he realized that she was no longer there in the studio with him. He had casually and unthinkingly covered that last of her exposed paintings with his own. For a long while, his breath caught in great heaving sobs, and the pain that he felt was unlike anything he had ever known – pointed, consuming, draining, unwanted yet somehow selfish. In that moment, surrounded by his work of the last year, he felt her absence more than he had in a very, very long time. Yes, he had often missed her intensely, but this time it was different. For the first time, she was truly gone...completely.

Slowly, Isaac Green gathered the frayed remnants of himself and walked into the house-proper. He pulled up a playlist on his phone, connected the Bluetooth speakers, and turned up the volume. Through the wall of Mahler, he cried hopelessly for nearly an hour and a half – he mourned his wife more powerfully than he ever had, but he mourned for himself even more. Alone separately? As evening came on, he arose, went to bed, and slept all night and into the next afternoon. He then pulled himself up, sat on the edge of the bed, and looked at the painting on the wall in front of him – Abby's only self portrait. He knew that he would eventually get through this, but he also had to admit to himself that he was, for the first time, lonely – truly and desperately.

Jean

(April 2019)

He hadn't laughed or smiled so much for years. The normally two-and-a-half hour drive took only about forty-five minutes – at least that's the way it felt to Isaac Green. He was surprised at how easy it all seemed. It had been nearly three years since Abby died, but Isaac had not since been able to imagine himself in any real relationship with another woman. And yet here he was in the car with Jean, headed to The Shack for a week.

Besides their chance encounters the previous fall and early winter, they had only gotten together twice. Isaac finally got up the courage to call her in February. They met at the A & D Cafe on a Saturday in early March for lunch, followed by a short hike along the river just outside of town. They talked about their pasts a bit, but Isaac Green didn't yet feel comfortable sharing how hard the last few years had been on him emotionally, so when it got a bit hard, he would switch the subject to his current home or writing projects, or he would ask her something about her work in the forest service. It was a wonderful afternoon. Just having someone to talk to and spend time with was good, but being with Jean was more than just that. He genuinely liked her, and he found her incredibly attractive – more so, the more time he spent with her. He liked her easy-going way, her voice, her laugh, her shape, her pretty face, and the way her hair hung alongside it. At the end of this date – yes, he thought of it that way – they hugged and set a dinner date for the next weekend. Before they separated, she leaned in, kissed him on the cheek, smiled, and turned quickly to head to her car.

They talked on the phone twice that week, making plans for their Friday night dinner. They decided that she would come to his house, and that he would cook steaks on the grill. She would bring dessert and wine. Isaac Green spent an inordinate amount of time on the preparations for the dinner. Besides a spring-cleaning-like attack on the house, he polished and detailed his truck, even though there was no reason to think that she would see it at all. His preparation for the meal was equally diligent; he purged his pantry and spice rack and replaced everything with fresher versions of the same items, he called the butcher twice to make sure that his filet mignons would be the best ones he could get, he organized the table settings several times, and he cleaned and polished the charcoal grill until it looked brand new.

Before she arrived that evening, Isaac was extremely nervous, fearing that he had forgotten something important. He hadn't. He heard her car door close and hurried to meet her at the door, which he opened just as she had raised her hand to knock on it. They both laughed at the old cliche of a movie scene. He welcomed her into the house by stepping aside and wave-gesturing her down the entry hall and into the living room. On the way in, she looked at everything on the hallway walls, and after handing off the pie and wine (two bottles) to Isaac, she made a huge, slow circle of the living room, fascinated by not only the artwork (mostly Abby's canvases) but also by the artifacts and furnishings. He was thrilled to find out that she seemed to have similar tastes as him in art, architecture, and decor. She insisted on a full tour of the house, which he gave with only minor trepidation at the doors to his bedroom and to the studio – his most personal spaces.

Back in the kitchen, the beautiful Meursault chardonnay she had brought initiated, then lubricated, the conversation. They moved from kitchen to living room to kitchen to patio to dining room, and she seemed to feel quite comfortable and at home. The meal was delicious – Isaac Green made a mental note to thank Steve at the butcher shop. After clearing, they decided to have dessert and coffee in the living room. He didn't remember telling her that peach was his favorite pie, but that's what she baked, and it was amazing. They sat next to each other on the couch, watching the fire dance and cast a glow over the room and them. Her face shone in its light, and he tried not to stare, but once she caught him doing just that, and she leaned in just close enough so that he recognized the movement as an invitation to kiss her, but only if he desired. He did, and they did. Though tentative and brief, it was gentle and delicious and full of promise for more, but at a future date.

During the next hour, they talked a bit, covering a wide variety of subjects, and they also sat in happy silence for extended periods. He asked about when they might get together again, and Jean said that she had to be gone all next week, as she had to go up to help with plans for a post-logging replant project up at the Rochester ranger station. Isaac Green mentioned that he had a cabin about a 30 minute drive from there, and that she was welcome to stay there if she hadn't booked a hotel yet. She hadn't, and she sat silent, thinking about his offer for a few minutes. She finally said, "What are *you* doing next week?" After a surprised second, he quickly thought ahead, then admitted that he had nothing planned. "I'll stay at your cabin, but only if you come, too." Her suggestion sent him reeling on the inside, and, a bit frazzled, he finally chuckled and said that it sounded like a great idea. Half and hour later, initial plans made, she got ready to go. At the door, she thanked him for a wonderful evening, and he could tell she was sincere. He had loved it, too. They hugged very warmly, and she trotted out to her car. When she had backed completely out of the drive and headed down the road, he closed the door. Smiling, he cleaned the kitchen, and poured himself a short whiskey to accompany the watching of the last of the firelight. He had not been so happy for a very, very long time.

As Isaac Green pulled the car up to Evelyn's barn, he suddenly realized that he had not contacted her, and she would know nothing about Jean and their growing relationship. How would she react to his being with another woman? Granted, they were not actually lovers (although he would have to admit to wanting that), he was here with someone who was not Abby, whom Evelyn loved like a daughter. A wave of panic and a sharp sense dread struck him, and it clearly showed on his face. Jean grabbed his arm and asked straightforwardly, "Are you all right?" He sighed, smiled, and explained briefly his sudden trepidation regarding Evelyn. Reaching over with both of her hands and, taking hold of his right one, she reassured him that it would be fine. Looking back into her shining eyes, he knew that she was right and said gratefully, "Thank you."

They got out of the car and headed toward the house. When they were still fifty feet away, the door flew open and Evelyn appeared in her kitchen apron, rosy cheeked from work and smiling brightly. She stepped toward them, and when they met, threw her arms around Isaac, drawing him into the depth of her most comforting of hugs. She had missed him, and he her. When he somewhat uncomfortably introduced Jean, Evelyn turned and grabbed her into the same encompassing embrace, whispering something into her ear that Isaac could not hear. The two of them continued back and forth for a full minute – their own private conversation. Isaac Green stood back and watched the interaction, which he thought strange, considering that they had just met. Evelyn of course, would not let them leave for the Shack without having them in for coffee and the completely predictable freshly baked treat – this time it was cinnamon rolls, which Isaac smelled before they even reached the threshold. He wondered how Evelyn remained so slim; she seemed to have baked something deliciously sweet literally every single morning, at least every morning that he had been there.

Conversation was mostly small talk and catching up on Isaac's kids, but Evelyn was also keenly interested in Jean's work, asking many questions and listening intently to Jean's responses. Isaac Green wasn't sure if she really was that interested in the work, or if she was somehow studying and testing Jean. Either way, the two of them seemed to get along famously. After an hour, Isaac insisted on getting started, as rain was impending, and he wanted to get to the Shack before it started. Evelyn carefully wrapped two more cinnamon rolls for them to take for the next morning. More hugs, smiles, and repressed tears; then they were off. Isaac saw Jean look back at Evelyn before they entered the woods at the trailhead. Following her gaze, he fleetingly saw Evelyn in her doorway, hand over her heart, with a look of what he could only describe as gratitude on her face. Jean smiled, and they stepped into the forest.

The hike to the cabin was fairly short, less than a half hour, and Isaac Green noticed that Jean was unusually quiet. Not that she was a big talker normally, but there was something slightly different in her mood. She seemed a bit distant, not really in a negative way – just sort of Mona Lisa-ishly sheepish. Eventually, he broke the silence. "What did Evelyn whisper to you when we first got there?" Jean smiled slightly, but didn't answer. Instead, she just looked directly at and into him for many moments. When she let go of his eyes, she suddenly picked up the pace down the trail, leaving him a few paces behind for a moment.

When they arrived at the Shack, he could tell that she was impressed. He had already told her about he and the guys building the cabin, perhaps underselling it. "You built this?!" Isaac nodded gratefully at the compliment, then unlocked the door and opened it. Shedding gear as he walked around the interior's main room, a combination kitchen and living room, he opened windows and turned things on and put things away. He went into the bedroom and opened that window. When he turned around, Jean was there, standing in front of the dresser, holding and studying the family picture of Isaac, Abby, and the kids from decades ago. He was frozen with discomfort, hesitation. Jean carefully replaced the photo on the dresser and continued to stare at it as she said, "Beautiful." He couldn't say anything, but just looked at Jean as she finally turned to him, a tear running down the right side of her face, and radiant with joy. She closed the two steps between them in an instant and kissed him passionately. Catching his breath, he opened his mouth to speak, but she put a finger to his lips and implored, "Please. Don't say a word." She kissed him again, even more intently, and began feverishly working to undo the buttons of her shirt.

Isaac Green woke up an hour later to find himself alone in bed, and he wondered for a few seconds whether he had only dreamed a beautiful dream, but as his consciousness grew, he became aware of sounds in the kitchen and realized that it was Jean, working on dinner. He got up, got dressed, and snuck into the bathroom to wash his face before joining her. He stood silently and watched her for a moment before announcing his presence. She looked beautiful, her back to him, wearing an oversized t-shirt and slipper-socks that pulled up over her calfs, her hair casually held with a clip into a short pony tail. He loved that she had found her way around the small kitchen and gotten things started. "Good morning," he joked as he approached. She gave a quick laugh and handed him a potato and a peeler, telling him to make himself useful.

They spent the rest of that rainy afternoon inside together – puttering around the cabin, doing the odd chore, sitting in front of the wood stove, making dinner. After eating and doing the dishes, they took some time reading with glasses of wine, music from his "Relaxing" playlist softly in the background. When a new song started, she nearly always commented, "Oh, I love this one!" or "Oh, I haven't heard this one in forever!" After about an hour, Isaac Green got up to stoke the wood burner, putting in a few larger pieces, and turning down the airflow to make the fire burn slower and longer. He also grabbed their empty wine glasses and took them to the sink.

Despite what happened earlier, he didn't want to assume anything about the sleeping arrangements. When they first arrived, he had planned on taking the loft bed, leaving the bedroom to her. Now he was unsure. They talked for a few minutes about plans for the next day. Jean didn't have to report to the station until Monday at 10:00 a.m., so he would have all day tomorrow to show her around the property and its environs. When plans were set, it was late, and clearly time for bed. She used the bathroom first, and he went in after, peeing, brushing his teeth, and looking at his awkward face in the mirror. When he stepped out, he stood uncomfortable outside the closed bedroom door for a minute, not certain about what to do. She made it easy for him by saying, "Are you coming? I'm a little chilly in here." She had lit the small oil lamp on the bedroom dresser, and as he stepped into the room, he could see by her exposed shoulders above the covers that she was naked under them. He carefully undressed and got in next to her, looking at her smiling and inviting eyes. This time, they took things much more slowly and deliberately, but just as passionately. They explored each other thoroughly, and he felt a sense of wonder and disbelief that he should find himself here, seeing, touching, and kissing her lips and body. She responded to and reciprocated every movement, and when, at last, they finished together, he held her close on top of him in a tight hug. When they had had a chance to catch their breath, he sensed her body relax, and could feel her smiling face on his chest. He wanted nothing more than to go to sleep like this, but just before they both drifted off, he was unexpectedly overcome by a rush of emotion. His breath heaved a bit, and he let out a slight sob, tears streaming from his own smiling eyes. She reached up and kissed his face, hugging him closer and whispering over a few times, "I know... It'll be all right." Her soft voice was the last thing he heard that night.

Sunday was beautiful and sunny, and Isaac and Jean hiked all over his property and into the Green Mountain National Forest to the east, as far as Gray's lake, where he often fished, swam, wrote, and painted. They laughed a good deal, talked a little, and simply walked together in comfortable quietness most of the time, sharing smiling, almost embarrassing, glances back and forth every so often. Isaac found himself thinking of Jean almost constantly, and he found that he was somehow magnetically drawn to her. They had made love at the Shack again in the morning, and now, just after noon, he wanted her again. He knew that it was ridiculous for him to feel and act so much like a teenager, but he had not felt this alive in nearly three years, and he didn't really care if he seemed foolish or not. After following her, watching her walk on the trail for about a half an hour on the way back to the cabin, he called her name, and she turned. Not waiting for him to say or do anything else, she strode quickly to his embrace, and they kissed feverishly. Finding their way off the trail and behind a large granite boulder, they sated themselves by kissing and touching – four hands moving simultaneously in an unchoreographed but somehow synchronized dance. Afterward, they both seemed surprised at their recklessness, but not ashamed. They felt like Adam and Eve here in this beautiful northern Eden – unflinchingly happy with each other, and open to whatever joys the day offered. That night, in bed, just as they were ready to drift off, she said at once jokingly and sincerely in another afterglow, "I'm really glad you decided to come with me up here." He was, too.

Isaac Green woke early and stole out to the kitchen to start making breakfast for them before Jean headed off to her week (really only four days) of work at the NFS ranger station up in Rochester. She would take his truck, and he would stay at the Shack, chopping wood, doing maintenance, and trying to get some writing done. When the coffee was ready, he woke her. She got showered and dressed while he finished making the pancakes and sausage. He liked the way she looked in her field uniform – a little more casual than her usual office wear, and a little more rustic. They ate and talked as if they had spent such mornings together for years. He walked with her back to Evelyn's barn, where his truck was parked. They kissed goodbye, and she took off, Isaac waving and watching until the truck was around the bend and out of sight. As he turned to head back into the forest, Evelyn came out from behind the chicken house, brushing feed crumbs from her apron. "I like her. You two seem awfully happy with each other." All he could muster was a "Yeah..."

Evelyn just laughed. "By God, you're blushing – a fifty-five year old man! Come on in and have a cup of coffee." Isaac Green just followed her in, but as he crossed the threshold, something came to him, and he adamantly shouted at her. "Fifty-FOUR!" The screen door slapped the jamb as he entered the kitchen. Outside, Evelyn's chickens clucked in the yard, and two big hawks chased and screeched at each other playfully in the blue sky above.

Observant

(May 2017)

When Isaac Green woke up this morning, it occurred to him that today might be a day of what he liked to call "intentional hiking." Most often, he hiked with a destination, with at least a rough plan of a route. At other times, hiking was for pure fun and exploration – he wanted to wander, play, and find new routes through fairly familiar territory. Then there were the occasional days like today, in which he consciously wanted to go at a much slower pace, becoming a real observer and student of the world around him. Isaac found that these hikes often filled his mental coffers with material for future stories or essays.

During intentional hikes, he carried binoculars and a real camera, one that could zoom further and catch things more clearly than his phone could. He also kept a small notepad and a pen in an outside pocket of his vest or jacket, ready to record anything that came to mind or vision. He remembered Hemingway writing that he would "hold an idea in his head" while he was hiking or fishing or killing a lion or having sex or whatever, but Isaac knew that he himself would do better to hold the idea in a notebook – it would likely get lost in his head. Throughout the early morning, as he got his coffee, breakfast, and shower, he continued to think about the day and decided that yes, he would intentionally hike a short section of the Monroe Falls Trail, a bit north and west of Branbury.

It only took him about fifteen minutes to dress, lace up, and pack his stuff, making sure that he remembered to gather the appropriate gear for his purpose today. He put in an extra bottle of water, as it would be a hot-ish day on trail, even at the slower pace. He arrived at the trailhead after a short twenty minute drive up into the mountains.

Monroe Falls was a really beautiful sight, and you could get a great view of it right from the parking lot and visitor's center. But the trail segment he would take, though a bit challenging, took you up and away and then eventually back to the very top of the falls, and it offered spectacular views of the valley below off to the east, including a panorama of part of Branbury to the southeast. At his arrival, only one other vehicle populated the parking lot aside from the visitor center attendant's Jeep. Isaac Green stepped into the center and asked the attendant in which direction the other visitors had gone; he was relieved to find that they had gone south – he was going west. The most difficult part of this trail began right at the first step out of the parking lot, a steep incline up granite steps cut and/or placed into the side of a prehistoric rockfall, now as stable as the stone wall high above. The top of this first ascent is where Isaac's intentional hike would begin – this first ten minutes, though, was just a chore.

At the top, Isaac Green sat on an outcrop, mopped the sweat from his brow with a bandana, and pulled out a water bottle. He forced his mind to calm as his gaze scanned the landscape below. His first impression was that he certainly lived in a beautiful area of the world; the forests which now dominated his vision were nearly perfect – hardly any diseased trees and hardly any sections that had been overlogged – and it seemed to go on forever. He let himself get lost in the immensity of it, smiling at his own tiny-ness. He wrote a quick sentence about this idea in his notebook under the heading, "Insignificance?" The question mark was an afterthought, but he was happy he put it in.

The trail continued south away from the falls, which became more and more of a whisper as he hiked on. As usual on these hikes, Isaac had to remind himself to slow down, open his eyes, open his ears, open his mind. As he did so, his breathing inevitably slowed and deepened. Almost immediately, he began to see things with a new clarity, both visually and mentally. The path passed through a brief but unusually thick stand of beech trees, and he wondered how old they were. He could usually guess within twenty years or so, but they were so densely packed together, they may be older than he would have otherwise thought, growing more slowly in the fight for sunlight. After another slight incline to the west, the trail topped-off on a ridge and would then slowly loop back around northeast and toward the falls once again.

Here on the summit of the ridge lay a beautiful Vermont mountain meadow, only about an acre in total, but desperately tranquil. As it was nearly summer, the wildflowers of spring had already begun to lose some of their colors, the purples, reds, and yellows now melding into a wider and heavier blanket of deep green, the color of life at its full strength. To Isaac Green, the change always seemed both affirming and melancholic. It gave him that Frostian "nothing gold can stay" feeling, which he'd experienced at many stages of his life, those transition points that everyone knows and which he knew all too well ever since last summer when he lost Abby. He left the trail to walk slowly through the not-quite-knee-high prairie of mixed plants. At the far side of the meadow, he found a downed tree, its clean horizontal trunk just asking to be sat upon; he obliged. After taking a drink, he closed his eyes and began again to slow himself. He heard the life all around him: the wind through the tops of the trees, and the creaking of the trunks and boughs bending to the breeze's will; the now very distant sound of the falls, which would gradually grow louder as he continued down the trail; the birds – jays, chickadees, nuthatches, and others – all making their diverse songs into a symphony penned by mother nature. It was a beautiful cacophony, and despite his attempt, Isaac had trouble writing it properly in his notebook. He crunched down a granola bar and took a few more big drafts of water. He picked and brushed the crumbs from the bar that had gathered on his shirt and lap into his hand, spreading them carefully on the log as he arose from it – coins to the busker birds for the concert he had enjoyed. Sad to leave this place, but anxious to proceed, he picked up the path and headed toward the sound of the falls at a self-imposed stroll.

The darkness of the forest surprised him a little as he stepped in from the meadow; it was almost as if he had flipped a switch or turned a dial to "dim." Everything was now much different and somehow more mysterious, the spare light sifting through, filtered, as thin strips of sylvan mist-cloth dropping white through the deep green background of the canopy. The temperature was at least ten degrees cooler here, and the air lay heavy as it hung down on him. Breathing was palpably more of a muscular event. Birds still sang in this sanctum of trees, but they were different birds, and their lower-pitched songs were more plaintive, pensive, and full of pauses. For several minutes, he watched as a pileated woodpecker hopped from branch to branch on a tree, and stutter-jumped around its trunk, but did not peck, though he seemed to be looking for a place to do so – its drumming would break the painful silence like a peal of laughter at the visitation for one's dearly departed aunt. He paused often, filling page after page of the little notebook. Despite the feeling of complete enclosure, Isaac Green somehow also felt at a greater distance to and from everything. Such was the power of the forest, and he made himself try to bear the weight as long as possible, slowing his pace even more. He recognized the timeless trope: Protagonist goes from the sunlit earth into the underworld, that dark night of the soul, hoping to survive and emerge changed and into a greater light and glory than he had ever before experienced. Isaac's dark night had begun nearly a year ago at Abby's hospital bed – why did he not, even now, want to deal with it once and for all so that he, too, could emerge into some semblance of newness or light? He wondered, had he become comfortable in his darkness, preferring a somewhat masochistic cocoon rather than facing the perhaps blinding light of the new unknown. He continued step-by-step through the deep forest.

The only real sensory difference throughout this long, dark forest crawl was that the sound of the falls inexorably increased in volume with each step. He knew that by the time he finally stepped out of the forest cover into the small glade near the falls, that it would be a roar – a huge wall of sound, not only in his ears, but in his face as well. An onslaught that you feel you have to lean into, as the TV weathermen do when they "bravely" stand out in the hurricane. As the sound nearly overwhelmed him, the forest began quickly to lighten, and Isaac Green found himself facing the glade that led to and overlooked the falls. His first step out into the opening put him in beautiful sun and a mottled but mostly blue sky.

Monroe Falls lay just below and in front of him, sparkling in the sun, each droplet screaming its joy as it dove from the last stones and over the edge, leaving a little bit of itself behind as a part of the great mist that gave a glow to the entire landscape. Everywhere Isaac looked had an iridescent gleam, and little rainbows dotted his entire range of vision. Discerning through the haze, he could see across the valley for miles, even to the far northern edge of Branbury. He spent some time in his notebook recording his observations and then his thoughts about them, all the while relishing the spectacle.

Finding a somewhat comfortable-looking rock propped up near the river right before it took the great dive, Isaac leaned back and closed his eyes for a few minutes before starting the trek back down. Feeling the wind pick up a bit, he opened his eyes and discovered that the sky had darkened markedly, and the clouds were moving heavy and quick above him. Without any more warning, they belched forth torrents of rain, soaking him to the skin before he had any chance of getting his rain gear out of his daypack – his priorities were to preserve his notebook and protect his camera. When he finally pulled out his rain jacket, it was too late to do him any good, so he wrapped it atop and around his pack, then stood, arms stretched up and out into the downpour. For several full minutes he simply stood there reveling in the warm early summer rain as a child might. Life is sometimes sunny, sometimes stormy, often surprising, and always enlightening.

On the hike back down, the differences in the landscapes seemed less contrasting than they had before. The light in the open areas was dimmer, and the birds were barely audible, in both the forest and the meadow. All the colors were muted by the rain and the clouds, blending into one nondescript military-drab green. He realized in retrospect that his intentional hike had finished when he scrambled to pack up his notebook by the falls. The downpour had forced him to become destination-bound again.   The stepping stones section of the trail was much more treacherous coming down in the storm than it had been going up but was still easier on his legs and lungs in descent – everything has its trade-offs. At the end of the day, Isaac Green had recorded some startling images and feelings from this intentional day, but he also came away with an idea about change being an integral part of all life. Though we may long for the comfort of what we had, and are often afraid to leave our spring and step ahead into seasons unknown, beauty and a rich harvest may indeed be found in the present, and hopefully even in what comes after. It may not bear the glorious sensory riot that preceded it, and it may be tinged with a kind of subtle sadness, but the idea of finding "comfort in melancholy" as he struggled to wade into the future was no longer just a song lyric for him, but the great truth of his now.

As Isaac Green reached for the handle of his pickup truck's door, he suddenly squinted and realized that the rain had stopped, replaced instantly, it seemed, by near-blinding sunlight. He smiled, shook his head, shimmied into the truck, and headed home to dry clothes, a review of his notes, and a beer.

Peace

(July 2019)

He kept his campfire smallish, intimate. Isaac Green felt even more private than usual tonight, and his pensive mood demanded an atmosphere of smallness, confined-ness, that a larger fire would not allow. Aging into his fifties, Isaac found himself often feeling nostalgic. Actually, nostalgia was not the right word for it, because he often spent more time in examination, questioning, and self-criticism than in longing for the "good-ole-days" – reflection might be a more accurate term. Now, watching the flames of the fire dance in its little arena of stones a few feet in front of him, he became drawn into himself and into an evaluation of his current life situation.

Past, present, and future always seemed to become intertwined and even confused in these reflections, as one inevitably influenced (at least the perception of) the other two. He had certainly lived a fortunate, even blessed, life thus far. His career, his marriage, his children, his second chance at life and love – these were all gifts for which he felt profound gratitude. Isaac hoped that he had always done right by Abby and the kids, and despite an ever-present sense of self-doubt and the strong sense of his own flaws, he would have to say that he thought he had done so – had at least tried. He also wondered if Abby would approve of Jean, and if he had taken enough time to grieve Abby before he found Jean – again, he hoped and thought so. Additionally, he tried to speculate what his life with Jean might be like in the months and even hopefully years to come. Would she tire of him, or would they grow into a comfortable and deep loving relationship that would sustain them both. These musings were typical of his reflections on such nights, yet even after he had come to reconcile his mind that his answers were satisfactory, he continued to explore the same questions over and over.

From the depths of his pondering, he looked up from the fire as a hushed sound and a bit of motion stole his attention. The underbrush at the edge of the forest just off to his left opened, and a medium-sized beautiful red fox vixen emerged from the woods at a trot. She stopped for a second to appraise him squarely, then scurried purposefully around the campground, sniffing at everything: around his tent, around the log where he had prepared dinner, at the air downwind of where he had hung the food bag, then finally around the fire and, hesitatingly back-and-forth, near and nearer still to Isaac himself. She even sniffed close to his outstretched legs and took a tentative and almost teasing nip at his socks just above his shoes. Evidently satisfied with what she had or had not found, she retreated a bit and positioned herself across the fire from Isaac Green, where she stood for a moment, and then lay down, regularly lifting her head to smell somethings on the breeze. Isaac had remained statue-still during the entire process, moving only his eyes to follow the fox through her circuit. For several minutes, the fox remained there across from him, their eyes looking directly one at the other. Finally, and apparently with no reason other than that she had stayed long enough, the fox stood and took one final look at Isaac, then turned and trotted without ceremony back into the woods from which she had emerged. Isaac Green, overwhelmed by thoughts and emotions, discovered to his surprise that he was weeping with happy abandon, and hugging himself to stop his heart from flying out of his chest. He sniffled a bit and blew his nose in a cotton bandana. He heard a sleepy, "Everything OK?" from inside of the tent. Clearing his throat, Isaac replied, "Yeah, fine. I'll be in in a little while. 'Night."

He sat there more than "a little while" longer, staring up at the clearing sky, watching the stars sift brighter through the gradually melting scattered clouds, and just breathing in the beauty of each more placid moment. The fire was no more than a visual whisper now, a few glowing embers, their eyes blinking dark longer and longer with each passing second, like a child finally giving way to sleep's call. His thoughts once again went to Abby, her striking face appearing in his mind as he closed his eyes for a moment. He whispered a barely audible, "Thank you...for everything," and it felt to him like an unwhispered "Goodbye" followed.

Several minutes later, he poured the remnants of his water on what was the fire, stood stretching in the not-quite-chilly night, glanced again at the now cloudless sky, looked wistfully to the woods, and strode to the tent. Exhaling a deep and satisfying sigh, Isaac Green curl-snuggled in with Jean. His drowsy eyes closed, and he felt his surrounding arm rise and fall over her deep, gentle breaths. Before he drifted off to join her in sleep, his final waking thought was that he had never before in his life felt a stronger sense of peace.

Made in the USA
Monee, IL
13 December 2023

48964392R00098